# MISSED CUE

# LYNN SLAUGHTER

ISBN: 979-8-88653-153-4

Melange Books, LLC
White Bear Lake, MN 55110
www.melange-books.com

Published in the United States of America.

Cover Design by Caroline Andrus

*For Alan*

# WHAT READERS ARE SAYING ABOUT MISSED CUE:

Don't let the title fool you. Lynn Slaughter doesn't miss any cues in this gritty mystery featuring a smart, ambitious, and emotionally flawed detective investigating the suspicious death of an otherwise seemingly healthy dancer. Set in the world Slaughter knows well, *Missed Cue* will keep you on your toes until the curtain drops on the final clue.

With *Missed Cue,* author Lynn Slaughter offers a riveting portrait of a female police officer on the trail of a killer and in search of herself. Watching Lieutenant Caitlin O'Connor unravel the case, as she seeks to better understand her own foibles, and help her alcoholic partner, made for an exciting read full of insight and suspense.

A delightful mystery that introduces an appealing sleuth with problems we all can relate to.

In *Missed Cue*, the star of the show isn't the dazzling ballerina Lydia Miseau, but the appealingly flawed police detective who investigates her murder. As Lieutenant Caitlin O'Connor begins the process of sifting through clues and interviewing suspects, she finds herself entangled in a double journey: to uncover both the identity of a killer and her own sense of self. Political scheming in the dance world is mirrored in her complicated relationships within the New Haven police department, and writer Lynn Slaughter renders both with precision and grace. Competing motives of fame, fortune, and family feuds all have their moment in the spotlight, but it's the backstage intrigue that propels this narrative to its satisfying conclusion. Well written and tightly plotted, *Missed Cue* is a showstopper.

LORI ROBBINS, AWARD WINNING
AUTHOR OF THE *ON POINTE* AND
*MASTER CLASS* MYSTERY SERIES.

Homicide Detective Caitlin O'Conner has a very full dance card: a murdered ballerina, a tango with a lover and a partner trying to tap dance around his problems. *Missed Cue* is a compelling story of a tough but vulnerable woman as she navigates her complicated life.

E.M. MUNSCH, AUTHOR OF THE DASH
HAMMOND SERIES, THE LATEST BEING *A
HAUNTING AT MARIANWOOD*

You'll be rooting for whip-smart detective Caitlin O'Conner as she searches for the killer of a star ballerina while also trying to untangle a complicated personal life. A stunning debut for the author's first adult mystery.

Lynn Slaughter is an expert mystery writer! The setting and atmosphere in Missed Cue create a strong hook that keeps us reading... Lydia, the beautiful, soulful ballerina of Ballet Études, collapses after swallowing the sleeping potion to fake her death as Juliet in Act III. Thus, the murder mystery begins. The clues are given, along with the false clues, and tension mounts as the stakes get higher. The sleuth, Lieutenant Caitlin O'Connor, maintains our interest: her partner is an alcoholic, and she herself is involved in an unhealthy love affair. Ms. Slaughter's details ring with authority... *Missed Cue* is a must-read!

Lynn Slaughter's latest tour de force, the suspense novel MISSED CUE, draws on her extensive background in the field of dance. The story opens in a rehearsal for the ballet *Romeo and Juliet,* and it is the perfect venue for a terrible crime. Lynn's seamless storytelling carries the reader right into the action, and she keeps us guessing as we meet all of her colorful and interesting characters. You should definitely pick up this book, but just be warned, you might not want to put it down!

CONNIE BERGSTEIN DOW, AUTHOR OF
*TAP AND RAP, MOVE AND GROOVE,* AND
OTHER BOOKS ABOUT DANCE

# PROLOGUE

Paul wiped the sweat off his forehead as he tried to keep up with the endless stream of lighting corrections Victor Pesetsky, Ballet Études' artistic director, screamed at him through his headset: "Slower fade! I don't want to be aware of the lighting change!" "For God's sake, she's supposed to look fourteen, not like an end-stage liver patient! Too much yellow." "You're losing her! Keep that spot on Lydia."

Paul chalked up Victor's edginess to pre-opening night nerves. In the seven years he'd been with New Haven's Ballet Études, Paul never failed to be moved by the magic Lydia and Alexander created when they performed together. And Lydia, beautiful, soulful Lydia, whose very presence gave him chills, had never danced with more assurance, or more convincingly imbued the role of fourteen-year-old Juliet.

Paul had lit dozens of ballets in his career and watched countless dancers in dramatic roles. He'd never encountered anyone who could more completely transform herself onstage than Lydia. After she swallowed the sleeping potion to fake her death in Act III, she danced with such despair and longing for her lover. Looking increasingly agonized, she stumbled about the stage until her collapse into slumber.

And then Paul's eyes widened. Lydia did something totally unlike her. She missed a cue, the musical cue to awaken. Paul leaned forward, unable to process what he was seeing. Darlene, the stage manager, crept onstage from her spot in the wings, frantically whispering to Lydia to get up.

The conductor looked confused as the orchestra played on.

"Cut!" Victor shouted as he strode down the aisle, and the orchestra stopped playing in the middle of a phrase. "God damn it, Lydia, what the hell?"

No answer. Darlene ran to the ballerina sprawled on the funeral bed. She gently shook her, but Lydia didn't stir. Darlene bent down, listening for a breath, a heartbeat. "Call 911," she screamed.

Paul ripped off his headset. Dizzy, so dizzy. He stumbled out of the lighting booth and clutched the stair railing to steady himself as he raced down to the stage. To Lydia.

# ONE

By the time Stan and I arrived at the theater, the stage area surrounding the funeral bed had been roped off. My chest tightened when I saw Chet Roberts, the medical examiner, who'd begun his preliminary investigation. Dancers, their faces wet with tears and streaked with ribbons of mascara, huddled in the wings. They reeked of sweat and hairspray.

"Please, no one leave," I said. "I'm Lieutenant Caitlin O'Connor, and this is my partner, Sergeant Stan Bisso. All of you take seats in the audience. I'll talk with you after I've checked in with the examiner." I turned to Stan and gestured for two of the patrol officers to join us. "Will you clear the dressing rooms and tell everyone to come sit out front? Seal off the deceased's dressing room."

The officers nodded. I knew I had to talk to Chet. My limbs felt unnaturally heavy as I headed over to him. Two nights ago, he'd ended whatever it was we'd had together. He said he couldn't leave his kids. Surely, I understood, didn't I?

I was trying, but shards of pain pressed against my heart. "Anything?" I asked in the coolest, professional tone I could muster.

He sighed and held his gloved hands up. Deep lines creased his forehead. His intense gaze latched on to mine. How many times had I gotten lost in those dusky blue eyes?

I forced myself to look away.

"No sign of a wound," he said. "Looks like heart failure. We'll know more when we get her on the table."

I nodded and knelt to examine the body. Lydia Miseau had been beautiful—delicate nose, high cheekbones, and coltish shapely legs. Her lean muscular frame reflected a lifetime devoted to the rigors of ballet. She didn't look like anyone ready to die.

I moved downstage toward the audience of dancers, orchestra members, and theater personnel. The work lights burned brightly. Rivulets of sweat worked their way down my spine. I shrugged off my jacket.

A sixtiesh-looking man wearing a fedora ignored the order to remain in the audience and clambered up the steps on to the stage. Splotches of red spread across his tear-streaked face. "I'm Victor Pesetsky, artistic director," he said, his voice trembling. "Lydia is my wife. She is in perfect health. I don't understand."

"I'm so sorry for your loss. You have my word that we'll conduct a thorough investigation."

"Thank you, but that isn't bringing her back. She is my muse, my soulmate." A fresh torrent of tears spilled down his face.

Must have been a May-December romance. Pesetsky was tall and gaunt, with piercing black eyes, a long, thin nose, and a shock of gray hair peeking out from under his fedora. My mother would have called him "distinguished-looking." Distinguished or not, he was clearly much older than his late wife.

A wiry guy wearing jeans and a black turtleneck joined us. "Oh God, oh God. I can't believe this. She was fine. This can't be happening."

"And you are?"

"Paul Gates, lighting designer. Lydia was my...my dear friend." His whole body shook.

Pesetsky stepped between us, as though he wanted to cut off Gates. I wondered if he wanted to claim his spot as Lydia's chief mourner, not this "dear friend."

"I'll need to talk with both of you," I said. "But first, I want to say a few words to everyone."

Gates turned to Pesetsky. "I'm so horribly sorry, Victor." He reached for his arm, and the newly widowed director swatted him away as though he were a pesky fly.

Hmmm. Something going on with those two? Or was Pesetsky just a prickly guy? Of course, his wife had just unexpectedly died. I'd known plenty of survivors whose grief took the form of angry irritation at anyone who tried to come close. Sure enough, rather than take a seat in the audience with Gates and the others, Pesetsky held himself apart, pacing up and down the side aisle.

Stan appeared. "Dressing rooms are all cleared. We roped off the deceased's."

I nodded.

Stan's perpetually sad eyes looked even droopier than usual. I had to admit Chet had nailed it when he said Stan reminded him of a Bassett hound, even though I'd felt defensive on my partner's behalf. "Hey, his wife dumped him for some rich banker," I'd said. "He's entitled to look a little down." Still, it was hard dealing with Stan's sadness, not to mention my own shit and the pressure of working homicide.

I shook my head. Time to focus. I walked over to the pale stocky woman wearing a headset. "You are?"

"Darlene Bott, stage manager."

"Do you have a microphone I can use?"

She grabbed a mike and handed it to me.

"And is there a place we can interview everyone individually?"

"Sure. We'll put you in the Green Room."

"That works." I moved to the stage apron to talk to everyone. A hush settled over the audience of dancers and crew, as though the curtain had just gone up, and I was the reluctant star of the show. I gulped. Nothing to do but get started. "Again, my name is Lieutenant O'Connor. I know this is a terrible shock. Ms. Miseau may have died from entirely natural causes, but we need to do a thorough investigation. Plan to stay here until we've had a chance to speak individually with each of you."

A few groans came from the evidently exhausted dancers.

I wiped the sweat off my brow. My blouse clung to my damp back. It was going to be a long night.

———

First was Victor Pesetsky, who slumped in and sank down on the lumpy loveseat as though he could barely hold up his long frame.

He heaved a heavy sigh. "I don't know what I can tell you, Officers. My wife was the picture of health. How could this have happened?"

I took the lead doing the questioning while Stan took notes. "We won't know until we get the results of the autopsy. Had she mentioned anything bothering her? Any sign that she wasn't feeling like herself?"

He shook his head. "No, nothing." He pulled his handkerchief out of his pocket and wiped his red-rimmed eyes.

"Were there any problems in your marriage?"

He stiffened and glared at me. "What are you implying? I was devoted to my wife, Detective. I resent any suggestion that I might have harmed her. She was my life, my muse."

"We're not implying or suggesting anything. It's our job to investigate."

He pointed a shaky finger at me. "That may be, but I would never have hurt Lydia."

"How about other people in her life? Did your wife have any enemies that you know of? Anyone who might have had a motive to want to harm her?"

"Of course not! Everyone adored her. She could easily have been arrogant because of her extraordinary talent. But she had the humility that only truly great artists possess. She was…one of a kind." He buried his face in his hands, and his whole body shook with noisy sobs.

*Was this an act for our benefit, or was the guy genuinely grieving?* I glanced over at Stan, whose raised eyebrows mirrored my own. After twelve years of working homicide together, we knew you could never discount a grieving spouse.

"I'm sure we'll have more questions for later, but that's enough for now. Again, we are so very sorry."

He nodded and took several heavy breaths as he mopped his face. He hauled himself up to standing and shuffled out the door.

Muriel Gaston came in next. She was impossibly tiny with doe-like blue eyes reddened with tears. "This is a nightmare," she said, as she dabbed at her face with a crumpled tissue. "Lydia was my mentor. She cared about all of us in the company. How could this have happened?"

"We don't know yet, but we're certainly going to do a thorough investigation to find out. So, Lydia was your mentor?"

"Yes. I was her understudy for Juliet, actually for most of her roles. She was thinking about retirement, coaching me so I'd be ready."

"And was she planning to retire soon?"

Muriel shrugged. "No idea. She talked about it, but she was dancing more beautifully than ever. She lived to dance."

*Hmm*, I thought. *And I bet you live to dance, too.*

"How long had you been her understudy?"

She pursed her lips. "Three years."

*Quite a wait for your chance to become the company star.* "That's a long time to be an understudy."

She shrugged. "I was learning so much from Lydia coaching me. I knew my chance would come. I didn't mind waiting."

*I bet.*

I shifted gears. "Can you think of anyone who might have wanted to harm her? Anyone she was having a conflict with?"

She shook her head. "Absolutely not. She was not only a brilliant dancer. She was genuinely a kind person."

And so, it went. By the time we'd done our last interview, it was after midnight. Hours and hours of interviews with folks who sounded like broken records. No, no one had seen or heard anything or anyone behaving suspiciously. No, Lydia had no enemies. Everyone revered her, not only as a great dancer but as a warm, caring human being.

Even Gus, the janitor, sang her praises. "You know how it is," he told us. "Some people act like you don't even exist. But Miss Miseau, she always greeted me. My wife's been real sick, and she'd ask about her, want to know how she was doing. She wasn't snotty like a lot of them."

"I could use a drink," Stan said as we packed up our stuff.

"Me, too. Charley's? Mind driving?"

"Sure."

———

By this hour, only a few stragglers remained at Charley's Bar and Grill, a regular watering hole for off-duty cops. We slid into a back booth. Marlene, the waitress whose fire-engine red hair always reminded me of Ronald McDonald, approached. We ordered a couple of Buds, and I asked her if the kitchen was still open.

"Nico's still here. He can fix you up. Long night, huh?"

"Yup." We ordered a couple of burgers with the works.

"Any preliminary ideas?" I asked Stan after Marlene headed to the kitchen.

He shrugged. "They were all singing the same song about her."

"Yeah. That really made me wonder. Maybe I'm jaded, but she couldn't have been all sweetness and light. One of my closest friends from high school was into ballet, and you wouldn't believe the stories she told me. It's so competitive. And Miseau had risen to the top. I doubt you get there just by being sweet. Plus, I saw her dance."

"You did?" Stan said, as Marlene set our beers down.

"Yeah. Last fall, I took my niece to see *Giselle*. Miseau was amazing. Talk about a fireball—she performed with such passion and reckless abandon. I don't think you can fake those qualities on stage. She had to be a lot more complicated."

"So, if she didn't die of natural causes, who do you like for this?"

I'd barely made a dent in my beer, and he was already signaling Marlene for another. *Oh God, here we go again.*

"Not sure. The husband's obvious, although he did look pretty torn up. Picked up some possible tension between him and the lighting designer. And then there's that Barbie look-a-like, Muriel Gaston, who's next in line for Miseau's roles. I'm sure there will be more when we investigate further."

Stan snorted. "Gaston's way too flat-chested for Barbie. I've never seen so many skinny women in one place. Do they ever eat?"

"I think so. But they probably burn it all off." Interviewing dancer after dancer had reminded me that no one would ever describe my big-boned five-eight frame as petite. Athletic maybe, but definitely not petite. I'd spent my life bemoaning the fact I looked nothing like my mom who was petite and delicate, not to mention gorgeous. I was sure everyone who saw us together wondered if I were adopted.

Marlene brought out our burgers, and Stan asked for another beer, and then said, "Hell, just bring me a pitcher."

Ever since JoAnne had left him, Stan's alcohol consumption had shot up on an express elevator. He didn't like me bugging him about it, but I had to try. He was my partner. I'd always had his back, and I needed him to have mine. Besides, I cared about him, loved him like a younger brother.

I put my hand over his. "I know you're hurting. But all this booze isn't helping. Not what you need right now."

He pulled his hand away. "Stay in your lane, Cait. My life's in the shit-can, and if a pitcher of beer helps me get through the night, well, so be it."

"Have you thought about getting any counseling?"

Stan slathered ketchup over his burger and shot me one of his "get off my case" looks. "Have you, Cait?"

I flinched. Apparently, he subscribed to the "best defense is a good offense" theory. But I wasn't about to launch a counter-defense. I knew I had a problem. "As a matter of fact, I've started seeing someone, a therapist. Maybe I can figure out why I keep falling for the wrong guys."

His head reared back. "No kidding. That's a step, Cait. Let me know how that works out for you... seriously."

"I will. But when we finish eating, I'm driving."

# TWO

The next day, Stan and I consumed an entire pot of coffee while we filled out paperwork and fielded media requests for comments about the sudden death of Lydia Miseau. Obviously hung over, Stan kept resting his head in his hands.

My stomach clenched. I wanted so badly to help Stan, but he'd created an impenetrable defensive wall. I ended up correcting several mistakes he'd made on the reports and wondered for the thousandth time whether I was making a mistake covering for him.

Just as I was about to call Chet to check on the autopsy progress, he texted me: *Found something interesting.*

I grabbed my jacket and stood up. "Going to see Chet. He's found something."

"You want company?'

"Nah. Take a break."

He smirked. I knew he was thinking I wanted to see Chet by myself. And maybe I did. No matter how much it hurt.

Thirty-five minutes later, I stood shivering in the morgue's examination room trying to ignore the acrid odor as I stared down at Lydia Miseau's body. And trying to ignore the swirl of emotions as Chet inched closer to me, as though daring me to move away from him. He knew how hard it was for me to resist his charm. He was such a beautiful man—smoky blue eyes, a tiny dimple on his left cheek I loved to kiss, and those long, graceful hands that had stroked me everywhere. I blinked. Hard. Focus. I had to focus.

"You're kidding," I said after Chet gave me the news.

"Nope."

"How far along?"

"Looks like around six weeks."

Victor Pesetsky certainly hadn't mentioned anything about a pregnancy. Had Miseau not told anyone—even her husband?

"So, what's the cause of death?"

He held his hands up. "I wish I could tell you. No external wounds. We'll have to wait on the toxicology reports, but as of right now, there's no evidence of anything that would have caused her death. It looks like her heart just stopped."

I gaped at him. "You're telling me you really have no idea?" The beginnings of a headache kicked in.

He gestured for me to follow him down the hall to his office. "The weird thing is her heart looks perfectly healthy. No evidence of scarring, and she was obviously in great physical shape."

"I can't believe this. So, she drops dead for no apparent reason?"

He licked his lips, lips that had scattered kisses all over my body. I forced myself to concentrate.

"There's always a reason, Cait. We just don't know what it is yet."

We entered his office, and I sank down on the seat across from his. I tried not to look at the picture of his adorable family prominently displayed on his desk—perky Marian and their two perfect children, Benjy and Crystal.

"You want some coffee?" he asked.

"No, I'm good. I may float away from all the cups I guzzled down this morning."

Silence hung heavy between us for several seconds. He ran his fingers through his hair and shook his head. "Look, Caitlin, I really am sorry about everything. I never meant to hurt you."

"Understood," I said, even as I thought, *"Isn't that what all dumpers say to dumpees?"* But what did I expect? Messing with a married man. Again.

"I can't bear to leave my kids, Caitlin. That's the bottom line. You know I love you. But I can't do this."

God, were those tears in his eyes? This was new. I stood up. "Hey, no hard feelings. I wish you only the best."

And I did. Mostly.

———

I picked up a chicken salad sandwich to go at Marco's deli and texted Stan to meet me at Ballet Études. The company's offices and studios were located in the same building as the theater, and I wanted to do some follow-up. Starting with Victor Pesetsky.

The marquee announced that the opening of *Romeo and Juliet* had been postponed until the following week. I met Stan in the lobby and filled him in on the news about Lydia Miseau's pregnancy.

His eyes widened. "Whoa. Didn't see that one coming."

Dora, the receptionist, a thirtyish-looking woman with tie-dyed hair and enormous glasses, directed us to the third-floor practice studio where Pesetsky was rehearsing with the company's male star, Alexander Varese, and Lydia's understudy, Muriel Gaston.

"Don't hesitate," he cried. Muriel ran and leapt into

Varese's arms, and he lifted her high above his head. "Good! Better. Now more, more. He is a magnet you cannot resist. You are helplessly drawn to him."

Interesting. Clearly, Pesetsky was wasting no time preparing his wife's successor as Juliet. Gone was the tearful, agitated man who'd seemed awash in grief. Today, he appeared totally caught up in coaching his wife's very young replacement.

We stood in the doorway and waited for a break. When the director's gaze landed on us, I detected a slight stiffening of his shoulders.

"Ah, Detectives," he said. "Any news?"

"The investigation is ongoing. We have a few more questions for you," I said.

Pesetsky gestured toward Varese and Gaston. "Take ten."

The dancers, covered in sweat, toweled off, guzzled water, and collapsed against the studio wall beneath the barre.

"Is there somewhere private we can talk?" I asked.

"Of course. Let's go downstairs to my office."

We followed him down three flights of stairs to the basement level. We passed a large costume and props room and rows of dressing rooms, including Lydia Miseau's, cordoned off with yellow tape.

Pesetsky ushered us into his small office at the end of the hall. Pictures of the company's signature productions lined his walls, several featuring Lydia. On his mahogany desk, I noticed a gilt-framed shot of his wife, as well as a photo of Pesetsky flanked by two thirtyish looking adults, a fragile woman, and a sturdy man with Pesetsky's distinctive nose.

"Are these your children?" I asked, as Stan pulled out his notebook.

"Yes. From my first marriage."

"And are they involved with ballet?"

"My son is actually our business manager, but my daughter has stayed as far away as possible. She lives in California. She and her husband are both corporate attorneys. She's seen the struggle of life in the arts."

"Were they close to Lydia?"

Pesetsky paused. "To be honest, not especially. They were teenagers when their mother and I divorced. Lydia was twenty-three, only a few years older than they were. They thought it was disgusting that I'd fallen in love with someone so much younger. But I couldn't deny my feelings. Sarah and I had grown apart, but my children were angry. At me and at Lydia whom they blamed for destroying their family."

"That must have been difficult."

He shrugged. "Well, truthfully, I have regrets about my relationships with my children. My son and I have grown closer in recent years, since he came on board to help us out with fundraising and finances. But my daughter? Not really. I suppose I've always been married to my art. I was much better at making ballets than I was at being a father."

He was being surprisingly forthcoming. And he'd just given me the perfect segue. "Mr. Pesetsky, were you aware that your wife was six weeks pregnant?"

He let out a heavy breath. "I take it you've seen the autopsy report?"

"Just the preliminary one."

"Lydia wanted to wait to tell the company until she'd gotten through the first trimester."

"How did you feel about the pregnancy?"

"I'm not going to lie to you. This baby was a surprise after sixteen years together. But we were…elated. Lydia is… was nearly forty. Dancers can't go on forever, and the baby coming…well, it changed everything."

"In what way?"

"Every year, my wife would say she was going to step down at the end of the season. And then after the last performance, she'd announce, 'Oh hell, let's go for one more.' And who was I to complain? She was still technically solid, and maturity had brought such depth to her dancing."

"But with the baby coming, you think she would have followed through on retiring for good?" I asked.

"I think so. The baby gave her something to look forward to, something to move toward."

"And for you?"

He rubbed his chin, then said, "This was going to be my chance for a do-over. Be a better father, a better man this go-round."

I stared at him as his face suddenly turned ashen. He brought his hand to his chest and shut his eyes. "Is there anything else, Detectives? I'm feeling a bit woozy." He reached down and pulled a bottle of pills and a water bottle out of his desk drawer. He shook two pills out and guzzled them down with water.

"Are you all right?" I wondered what he was taking.

"I will be. Anything else?"

"Just a couple more questions. Was your wife's life insured?"

"Yes, of course. We insure all our principal dancers. Our audiences come to see these magnificent artists. If something happens to any of them, it's a major loss for us at the box office."

I pressed on. "But you weren't concerned your wife was planning to retire and become a mother? Wouldn't that have hurt the box office?"

He shrugged. "I love my wife. We both knew she could not dance forever. And we were preparing. She was working closely with Muriel—grooming her, I suppose you might say, to take over her roles. My wife is a wonderful coach. And Muriel is a sponge, a great talent as well."

*Mighty convenient to have a ready replacement for your dead star.* "So, how much was Lydia's life insured for?"

Victor stood up and waved his hand. "I can't recall. My

son, Frederick, handles all of that. Now, if you'll excuse me, I really must get back to rehearsal." He moved toward the door, then turned around. "Have you learned anything about what caused my wife's death?"

"Nothing definite," I said. "We're waiting on the toxicology report."

"My wife did not take drugs, Detectives. She was in perfect health. I strongly doubt your toxicology report will show a thing."

"We'll keep you informed." As he walked out, I couldn't help wondering why he seemed so confident the toxicology report would reveal nothing.

# THREE

O ur next stop was three doors down, the even tinier office of Frederick Pesetsky, a younger, shorter, and burlier version of his father. He was on the phone when I tapped on the frame of his open door. He motioned us in. "Look, we'll pay you as soon as the funding from the Arts Council comes in...Yes, I know we're overdue. I'm asking for your patience. You do know we're dealing with the tragic death of our principal dancer, don't you?" Frederick listened for several seconds, then reiterated that he'd be in touch soon and clicked off.

He rubbed his forehead. "Creditors. They couldn't care less what we're going through. The joys of being in the arts. So, what can I do for you, Detectives?"

"Your father mentioned that Lydia's life had been insured by the company," I said.

"That's true. We insure all the principal dancers."

"Mind telling us how much her life was insured for?"

"As I recall, it was a lot. Let me look this up for you." He began typing on his laptop.

While we waited, I checked my phone for texts. Nothing, except for messages from reporters begging for a quote.

"Wow," the younger Pesetsky said. "I didn't recall it was that much, but of course, she is the company's star."

"So, what are we talking about here?" I asked.

"Ten million."

"That's a lot of money. How serious is the company's financial situation?"

"Off the record? Very serious. We were worried we'd have to lay off some of the corps dancers." He pushed his chair back and shook his head. "Ballet is expensive to produce, and for the past three years, the Arts Council budget has been slashed. Every arts organization in the city is feeling the pinch. People don't understand that ticket sales only cover a portion of our expenses."

I nodded. "I take it then that this insurance money will be very helpful."

He looked pained. "Well, I suppose, but what an awful price to pay for financial solvency. Lydia is...was my father's muse—a genuine star with a huge fan base."

"How did you feel about her?'

He shrugged. "At first, I hated her. I was only fifteen when my father abandoned our family for her. His betrayal nearly killed my mother. And Lydia was so young. But over the years, I think we both softened. I could see she wasn't the devil—just someone very ambitious. And incredibly gifted."

Frederick Pesetsky was poised as he spoke, almost as though he'd rehearsed his lines. But was he being entirely truthful about his feelings toward Lydia? The father of Melissa, my closest childhood friend, abandoned his family for another woman when she was a teenager. Now in her upper thirties, she'd confided she still harbored revenge fantasies toward her father's paramour. Had Frederick had similar fantasies and opted to act on them? He had an additional incentive, after all. As the financially struggling company's business manager, wouldn't he relish adding ten million dollars to the company coffers?

I nodded, and then asked, "Were you aware Lydia was pregnant?"

Frederick's mouth gaped open. "You're kidding."

"No."

"That won't be good news for my father."

"Why not?" I asked.

"Well, for one thing, he's not in great health—don't know what he'd do without his nitroglycerin. Besides…" He paused, as though debating about whether he should continue.

"Besides what?" Stan asked.

"I overheard my parents arguing about having more children before they split up. My mother wanted another child, and my father flatly refused. He could barely tolerate the ones he had."

God, he sounded bitter, and why wouldn't he? I pressed on. "And yet you're now working with your father."

He shrugged. "Now that I'm an adult, we get along much better. I grew up watching ballet and fell in love with it. I'm in a position to help sustain it. And frankly, I'm useful to my father."

Interesting choice of words, I thought. So, the way to become more than "barely tolerated" was to be "useful" to his dad's ballet company.

Stan and I thanked him for his time and slipped out of his office. As we walked down the hall, I thought about Frederick's simmering resentment toward his father. He'd claimed they were now getting along much better, but what if he couldn't resist a little payback toward dear old Dad by arranging the elimination of his mother's replacement? Moreover, the insurance money would dramatically improve the company's financial footing, a definite plus for its business manager.

And then there was Victor Pesetsky. He was either a hell of an actor or a changed man in his later years. He'd made a point of telling us how elated he was about the coming baby and how much he was looking forward to another shot at fatherhood. Given his lousy record as a parent and his total devotion to his artistic work, how "elated" was he?

Moreover, Victor knew about the insurance money and must have known it would help the company dig out of its financial morass. Yes, he'd lose his star, but Muriel Gaston seemed more than ready to take her place.

How ready? It must have been hard to wait in the wings to become the company's leading dancer while Lydia put off retiring year after year. She could have decided to hasten the ballerina's exit. Definitely worth talking to her again. "Let's head back up to the studio and see if we can catch Muriel Gaston."

Stan nodded. "Good idea."

We were almost there when the third-floor doorway creaked open, and Muriel Gaston and Alexander Varese appeared, looking flushed and weighed down by their dance bags. Funny how dancers often looked so tall and imposing on stage, and in real life, were often on the diminutive side—like these two.

"Ms. Gaston," I said. "We have a few more questions."

Her crystal blue eyes widened. "For me?"

"Yes. Is there somewhere we can talk privately?"

"Sure. We can go to one of the women's dressing rooms. The other dancers are off today."

Five minutes later, Muriel Gaston was settled on a lumpy pea green loveseat in the corner of the long, narrow mirrored room. Stan and I sat across from her in chairs we'd pulled up from the makeup table that lined the wall. A pile of old *Dance Magazines* lay on the floor near Gaston. She pulled off her pointe shoes and winced as she rubbed her feet with an oint-ment that smelled strongly of menthol. "Long rehearsal," she said.

"From what we saw, your practice went well," I said.

"Yes—I mean, under the circumstances." She sighed. "I still can't wrap my head around Lydia being gone."

"I can only imagine. How did you feel about her?"

She abruptly abandoned her foot massage and stared at me. "Like I said last night, she was an extraordinary dancer and a wonderful human being."

"Did it frustrate you that she kept putting retirement off?" Stan asked.

She pursed her lips and shrugged. "Sometimes. I'm not going to tell you I didn't want the chance to dance Lydia's signature roles. But you have to understand, I was learning so much from her. Lydia believed in me, told me all the time I would someday surpass her as a great ballerina. She helped me to believe in myself. And anyway…" She paused.

"Anyway?" Stan prompted.

"A few days before… she died, she told me she would soon have a surprise for me, news that would make both of us very happy. And then she pulled me into her arms." Her face clouded over, as she lifted a shaky hand to her bun and shoved back a loose hair pin.

"Did you have any idea what she meant?' I asked. "What the surprise was?"

She shook her head. "Of course, I wondered if she meant she was retiring, but…"

"Go on," I said.

"If the surprise was her retirement, I couldn't fathom how that would make her happy. Lydia lived to dance."

"So, you didn't think her retiring was the surprise?" Stan asked.

She frowned and shook her head. "No, that's just it. I think this time, she was serious about stepping down. For the last several weeks, our coaching sessions were long, intense. She pushed me hard—brought things out of me I didn't even know were there." Her voice shook as she added, "I will be indebted to her forever."

"Is there anyone else she was especially close to that we should talk to?" I asked.

She wrinkled her nose, as though she'd just tasted something dreadful. "Try Paul Gates. They were very close."

We thanked her for her time and headed out. On the ride back to the station, Stan said, "Did you get the feeling she was implying Miseau and Gates might have had a thing going—and she wasn't thrilled about it?"

"Yup. Let's pay him a visit on Monday."

"You think Muriel Gaston could have had anything to do with Lydia's death?"

"I don't know, Stan. She seemed to be genuinely grieving for her mentor. If Lydia was murdered, Gaston doesn't appear to be a promising suspect. Then again, we've both been on the job long enough to know appearances can be deceiving."

# FOUR

Frederick Pesetsky sat in his office stewing about his father withholding information from him—information he couldn't believe those nosy detectives had blindsided him with.

He headed down the hall to his dad's office and entered without knocking. "When were you planning to tell me, Lydia was pregnant?"

Victor startled and then slumped in his chair. Still in his rehearsal clothes, he mopped his face with the towel wound around his neck. "Give it a rest, Frederick. It doesn't matter now."

"Doesn't matter? You've had a vasectomy, for God's sake. The police are sniffing around like they can't believe their good luck identifying your strong motivation to off your wife. Now it's not just the insurance money, but the fact she was obviously cheating on you."

Victor's nostrils flared. "If you're implying I would harm my wife, I'm insulted. I could ask you the same thing. I know you resented Lydia, always took your mother's side."

"That's ancient history. You know perfectly well I could never kill anyone, not even your cheating child bride."

"Don't talk about her that way! And as a matter of fact, Son, until they figure out her death was from natural causes, the police must be taking a hard look at you as well. There's no question that the insurance money would get us on more solid financial footing."

Frederick sank down on the armchair across from Victor and ran his hands through his thinning hair. "I've busted my balls trying to hold this company together financially. And yes, the money's going to help. Not that we'll see a penny until this thing gets sorted out... But surely you know I could never harm Lydia. And I still don't understand why you didn't think I was worth your letting me know what was going on. It was Gates, wasn't it? All that stuff about what great friends they were was a bunch of bullshit."

He nodded. "Lydia's...indiscretions were not my favorite topic. We had decided to stay together. Once she got through the first trimester, I was going to tell you, tell everyone, about her pregnancy."

Frederick shook his head. He hated feeling like an outsider in his father's life. "I wish you'd trusted me."

"Try to understand." Victor's eyes misted over. "I felt so humiliated. I divorced your mother, destroyed our family, all for Lydia. I never imagined she'd betray me like this."

Frederick stared at his father, who looked so worn... and old. His anger evaporated. "I really am sorry, Dad," he said before slipping out the door.

# FIVE

Saturday morning, I did my usual three-mile run, showered, and spent the rest of the day cleaning my apartment and shopping for groceries. My mind ricocheted between mulling over the case and mourning the departure of Chet from my life. When was I going to learn that love affairs with married men never ended well? What the hell was wrong with me?

Saturday night, I inhaled three slices of takeout pizza followed by an entire pint of Ben and Jerry's chocolate chip cookie dough, my go-to comfort food. I fell asleep on the couch watching a Lifetime movie and nodded off before the happy ending. Just as well.

I was startled awake by someone pounding on my door. I glanced at the clock. 3:00 a.m.? What the hell? I grabbed my Glock and headed for the door where I peered through the peephole. Chet stood there, his sandy blonde hair a disheveled mess. I undid the chain and flung open the door.

He stumbled in and grabbed me as though I were the last lifeboat on the Titanic. I breathed in the distinct scent of Scotch. A lot of Scotch. "What are you doing here, Chet? It's three in the morning."

"I know, I know," he said. "I'm sorry. I had to see you, hold you. Let's sit down, okay?" He moved to the couch and patted the seat next to him.

I shook my head and remained standing. "What happened to 'I can't see you anymore, I have to work on my marriage'?"

He ran his hands through his hair. "I thought I could do it. But I don't know how to stop loving you, wanting you."

"I'm not a Goddamn yo-yo, Chet. You can't fling me down and then pull me back in again. It's too hard. It hurts too much." I took a deep breath and willed myself not to cry.

"You're right. I know I can't keep doing this to you, to us. I keep thinking about that line from *Brokeback Mountain*, 'I wish I could quit you.' That's how I feel, like I want to make a clean break, do the right thing, but I can't make myself."

"Maybe you're not trying hard enough. It hasn't even been a week."

"And I'm already in hell. I need you."

"Need me for what? You have a wife, who's probably wondering right now where you are."

"She's not here. Took the kids to see her sister in Jersey."

"So that makes this okay?"

"No." He stood up and moved toward me. "But the only thing that feels okay is being with you, loving you. Please, let me hold you, just for a minute."

I hesitated. I should tell him to get out, leave me alone. But I couldn't do it. I wanted him to touch me. He wrapped me in his arms and buried his face in my neck. We stood there, swaying, like a couple of storm survivors clinging on to one another.

He whispered in my ear, "Tell me you don't want this, don't want me, and I'll go."

"You know I can't do that," I said, before I led him into my bedroom.

———

Chet spent the night and ran out to get us bagels and the Sunday *Times* the next morning while I brewed a pot of coffee and listened to some Wynton Marsalis. We settled across from one another at my tiny, gnarled kitchen table. Except for my Newport Jazz Festival posters, everything in my apartment came from consignment shops and Goodwill. Nothing matched, and I liked it that way.

"You look so beautiful," he said. "You know, when I'm home. I can't even bear to watch *Law and Order: SVU* because it makes me miss you so much."

"What in the world are you talking about?"

"That police captain. She reminds me so much of you—tall, voluptuous, gorgeous."

"If you mean Mariska Hargitay, I'm flattered, but no way am I in her league. She's a goddess."

"So are you. I wish you could see yourself the way I see you. And I wish we could be together like this… in the morning, I mean. Every day."

"Me, too. But that's not how it's going to go, is it?"

He closed his eyes and his face sagged. "I wish I knew," he mumbled. "I feel like such a dick. I shouldn't have come."

"I shouldn't have let you stay, so we're even."

———

After Chet left, I spent the afternoon in the basement doing laundry, trying unsuccessfully to focus on reading through the *Times*, and beating myself up over letting Chet back into my life. Being with him was like a drug. When we made love and he held me afterward, telling me over and over how much being with me meant to him, I felt satiated, high on being so wanted, needed. But once he was gone, the euphoria wore off quickly, and all the side-effects set in—the hollowness, the emptiness. And the guilt.

———

Monday morning, Stan arrived at work forty-five minutes late, looking bleary-eyed. His nose had taken on a reddish glint, and the mouthwash he must have guzzled couldn't quite eliminate the odor of stale beer.

"You look like hell," I said.

"How I feel. Long weekend, you know?"

"I do. Look, Stan, it's not even nine o'clock in the morning, and I can smell beer on you. You need help. How about if I go with you to an AA meeting? Morty's been sober for two years. He says there's a good meeting at the Y on Monday nights."

His face darkened. "You been talking to Morty about me?"

"Of course not. You know he talks to anyone who'll listen about being in recovery. I didn't say a word about you."

He slumped into his seat. "And let's keep it that way. Look, I know you mean well, but I have this under control. Honestly, it's just a rough period. JoAnne called on Saturday and told me she's getting married to that dick at her bank."

Our desks faced each other, and I reached over to touch his arm, but he waved me off. "I'm really sorry, Stan. This totally sucks."

"Yeah, well, she's finally going to have the lifestyle she always wanted. The guy drives a fucking Porsche."

"Definitely above our pay grade. But you know what? She threw away a great guy."

"Don't think she sees it that way."

"Her loss. Come on. Let's go track down Paul Gates after we hit Starbucks. My treat."

———

Forty minutes later, we found Gates in the lighting booth at the theater, programming lighting cues. Dark circles rimmed his eyes. I wondered if the guy had slept at all.

"Making changes?" I asked.

"Always. Victor gave me a ton of notes just before...well, you know."

"I do," I said. "Do you have some time to talk to us?"

"Sure. But I don't know what else I can add that I didn't tell you the other night. Lydia was a beautiful human being, inside and out."

I nodded. "Muriel Gaston mentioned that the two of you were very close."

He stiffened. "She did, huh? Well, that's true. Lydia didn't have a lot of people she felt comfortable confiding in. But we'd known each other for years. She trusted me, knew that whatever she told me stayed with me."

"I take it you knew that she was pregnant."

He hesitated. "I did."

"Did she say anything about how she felt about expecting a child? Her marriage?"

"Two different questions, Lieutenant. She was shocked when she discovered she was pregnant, and then she grew excited, almost euphoric. Her career as a dancer was inevitably nearing an end, and a child seemed like a new beginning."

"And her marriage?" Stan asked.

He held his hands up. "She was determined to make it work. Her parents had split when she was a baby, and she didn't want that scenario for her own child."

"Understandable," I said. An image of Chet talking about his kids and how he couldn't bear to leave them flashed in my mind. I pushed it away.

"Were there problems in the marriage?"

Gates knitted his hands together and pressed them against his chin. "Since she's gone, I guess I can tell you. In a word, yes. Lydia told me she didn't think Victor was actually in love with her, but rather, with her dancing."

"What did she mean?" I asked.

"At home after the first year or two of their marriage, he more or less ignored her. She used to say the only time she could get his attention was in rehearsal, where he fawned all over her as a dancer, his mighty muse. Honestly? Lydia was the loneliest person I'd ever known."

I felt a rush of empathy for Lydia Miseau. The picture I was getting of Victor Pesetsky was of a single-minded man, obsessed with the art he was making. Like Frederick, Lydia had apparently felt valued mainly for her usefulness to him.

Was that what I was to Chet? Someone useful? A respite from the pressures of raising young kids and pleasing a wife who obsessed over redoing their living room? I brushed the thought away, as Stan jumped in with a follow-up.

"Did you agree with her that she should stay with Victor if she was that unhappy?"

He hesitated. "No. But it was not my call. Lydia had a will of steel. She was going to make this work and not put her child through what she'd gone through growing up with a stressed-out single mom."

"When we spoke to Ms. Gaston, I got the impression that you might have been more than close friends with Lydia. Were the two of you involved?" I asked.

He shook his head. "Not like that. Look, Muriel and I used to be a couple. When I broke things off, I think she thought it must be because I'd found someone else. And like I said, Lydia needed someone to talk to, and I was that person. Muriel wrongly assumed more was going on than there was."

"Anything else you'd like to add?" Stan asked.

He shrugged. "Can't think of anything. She was one of a kind." His eyes misted over as we thanked him and stood up to go.

———

Walking back to the car, I said, "Did you get the vibe that he wasn't being entirely truthful when he told us there was nothing going on beyond friendship?"

"So far, my feeling is that nobody we've talked to is coming entirely clean with us. Not Gates, and not Frederick, who claimed he'd gotten over his hatred for Lydia—and definitely not Victor, who wanted us to believe he was excited about his wife's pregnancy."

"No kidding. And we still don't know what killed Miseau. I'm going to drop by Chet's office and check on toxicology updates. You want to come?"

"Nah. When I'm with the two of you, it reminds me of what JoAnne was doing with her banker guy behind my back all those months."

I winced. "Stick the knife in me, why don't you?"

He shrugged. "I'm calling it what it is, Caitlin. What you're doing isn't cool."

I let out a heavy breath. "I know."

# SIX

I dropped Stan off at the station and spent the twenty-minute drive to the medical examiner's office fuming about what he'd said. How dare he? I'd never asked Chet to leave his wife. I was no home wrecker. It wasn't the same situation at all. And where did Stan get off on judging me when he was drinking himself to death?

When I pulled up in the parking lot and switched off the ignition, I sat there, drumming my fingers on the steering wheel. Was Stan the one I was mad at? Or was it me? What was I even doing here? I could have called Chet for updates. I couldn't even be honest with myself. I wanted to see him. What was it Victor had said the other day in rehearsal to Gaston? Something about "Romeo" being her magnet. For better or worse, Chet was mine.

I found him in his office typing notes on his computer with those long, graceful fingers of his. Once he'd told me his childhood piano teacher thought he could have a career in music. "Those hands," she'd said. I could believe it.

When he saw me, his face lit up. "This is a pleasant surprise, Lieutenant," he said.

I slipped into the office chair across from him, determined

to remain professional. I was on duty, for God's sakes. "Here on business. Checking to see the status of the toxicology reports on Lydia Miseau. You have anything for me?"

His smile evaporated. "I wish I did. All of the tests aren't back yet, but the ones that have come in show nothing in her bloodstream. Zilch. This has really got me stumped. All of her organs check out as healthy. Her heart just stopped beating."

I sighed. "Why do I feel like I'm on a bad episode of *Unsolved Mysteries*? This is so frustrating."

"I'm right there with you."

"Keep me informed as soon as the rest of the tests come in. My gut tells me someone close to her helped her die, but I have to know cause of death to move forward."

"Understood. You know you can count on me to keep working on this until I figure it out. And Caitlin?" He got up and shut his door. "I want to apologize to you for the other night. I'm having a really hard time letting you go."

He reached for me and pulled me up to standing and into his arms. I inhaled the familiar scent of his Old Spice after-shave before I pulled away. "I can't do this, Chet, and I can't not do this. I've gotta go."

I slipped out the door before I could change my mind and engage in something entirely unprofessional while on duty.

———

That night, I went over to Melissa's for dinner. She'd been my closest friend ever since ninth grade at Sacred Heart Academy when we both got cast in *You Can't Take It With You*. We did theater together all through high school. Melissa was the real star though—she had this amazing voice and presence. Still does. I thought she should go on to act, but instead, she became a middle school language arts and drama teacher. She's the only person I've ever met who claims to love teaching middle school.

She and her husband Ronnie and their three kids had a sprawling two-story brick home in one of the newer subdivisions in Branford. Wall-to-wall kids and families lived on their block, and every yard had a swing set. It was like stepping into a different universe.

When I pulled in the driveway, Barry and Isabel, Melissa's two oldest, along with Ralph, their Scottie, scampered out to greet me. Three-year-old Maddie toddled out behind them, yelling "Aunt Caitlin!"

I hugged all of them and pulled out the treats I'd brought —Barry's favorite, a giant Kit-Kat bar, a Nestle's Crunch for Isabel, a Hershey's milk chocolate for Maddie, and a milk bone for Ralph. "Whatever you do, don't tell your mom I brought you these," I said.

They immediately ran in ahead of me to give me up to their mom.

"So," she said, pulling me into her arms, "once again, you couldn't resist. Our dentist is not going to be happy with you."

I laughed. "Guilty as charged. How are you?"

"Long day at school. The kids are more than ready for spring break, and so am I. But I'm probably doing better than you are. I've been reading about that ballet dancer's death. How's the investigation going?"

"Not great. We still can't figure out the cause of death."

Ronnie emerged from the kitchen carrying a tray loaded with a bottle of Chardonnay and three glasses.

Melissa jumped up and gave him a kiss. "You're the best."

And he was. I'd known Ronnie since our sophomore year at UConn when he and Melissa got together. He was totally devoted to her and the kids. He set the tray down and came over and pecked me on the cheek. "How ya' doing?"

"The usual. Glad to be with you guys. And this guy." I gestured to Ralph as we all settled in the living room. I bent down to pet him as he chewed noisily on the bone I'd brought him.

Melissa poured the wine and handed us glasses. After about five minutes of "boring grownup" talk, the kids descended to the basement playroom.

"Call us when dinner's ready," Barry said.

"Absolutely no eating candy until after dinner," their mom yelled down to them in her best middle school teacher's voice.

The sound of giggling was her only response. Melissa glared at me. "See what you've done?"

"I know, I know. I'm a terrible influence, but you love me anyway."

"That's the truth."

We talked about the family trip they were planning to Disney World over spring break, Ronnie's insurance business, and the latest intrigue at Melissa's middle school where three eighth-graders had gotten caught spiking the punch at the Valentine's dance.

"Where'd they get the booze?" I asked.

"Where do you think? Mommy and Daddy's stash at home."

"Well now, from what I've heard, you girls pulled a few pranks in your day," Ronnie said.

I grinned. "Remember the time we set the clock forward thirty minutes in Sister Mary's class, and she let us all go ahead of time? Boy, was she mad when she figured it out."

"Those were the days when there were blackboards, and we had to clean every one of them after school for a week." Melissa looked at me. "Totally worth it," she said.

"So, what smells so good?"

"Your favorite—chicken cacciatore."

I clutched my chest. "Be still my heart. I'm salivating."

Ronnie got up and headed for the kitchen. "Going to go check on things." Melissa not only snagged one of the nicest guys on the planet, but his hobby was cooking.

She leaned toward me. I knew what was coming. She was

going to ask about my love life. Sure enough, she said, "So what's the latest on you and Chet?"

For the millionth time, I wondered why I'd ever told Melissa about him. But how could I not? She was my closest friend. I bit my lip. "Sort of the same, and sort of not. Last week, he told me it was over, and he was going to work on his marriage. But that only lasted for a few days. I feel like an addict."

She frowned at me. "What does your therapist say?"

"We've only met once. Going again this week. We haven't gotten into it much yet."

"You need to tell her this isn't the first time. And you deserve so much better."

"Do I? I must not." I looked around her comfy living room with the overstuffed chairs and kids' toys strewn everywhere. God, I envied my best friend. But I couldn't imagine my crazy life as a homicide detective meshing with a family needing attention.

"That's ridiculous. You're smart, kind, and you're gorgeous. You don't need to settle for being some married man's leftovers."

I stared at her, not smiling. I hated being called someone's "leftovers." Even if it was true. "Can we change the subject? I really am going to work on this in therapy. I promise."

She huffed. "Well, it's about time."

Ronnie called out, "Dinner," and I took off for the dining room before Melissa could say one more word about my problem. I loved my friend dearly, but she was the original "Ms. Fix-It," and she'd been determined to fix me for years. So far, so not good.

———

My brain didn't want to turn off that night, as I thought about the case. And Chet. Always Chet. I finally drifted off sometime around midnight. Less than an hour later, my phone rang. I picked up on the third ring. "O'Connor," I mumbled, hoping I wasn't getting called in to work for an emergency.

For several seconds, all I heard was breathing. Heavy breathing.

My heart thumped in my chest. "Who is this?"

A distorted voice that sounded like Darth Vader on crack said, "You don't deserve to live."

"Identify yourself," I demanded.

The caller clicked off.

God damn it! I checked the last call button and got the "number unavailable" message. I'd talk to Nick, our technical guy, tomorrow to ask if there was any way to trace the number. I racked my brain for who might have it out for me and came up blank. Sure, I'd helped put away quite a few murderers, but Bridgeport's Correctional Center didn't allow inmates to make threatening phone calls. And how would they have gotten my number, anyway?

No, it had to be someone closer, someone I knew personally. I shivered and padded over to my door and double checked the lock. Then I climbed back into bed and huddled under my comforter, my gun under my pillow. Sleep eluded me for a long time.

# SEVEN

I felt like total shit the next morning. And it didn't help that when I got to work, Stan called in sick. "Some kind of a stomach thing," he told me, his voice slightly slurred. Translation: He had a hell of a hangover.

"How much did you have to drink last night?"

"I tossed back a few, but that's not the problem. It's that stomach virus going around."

"Right. Look, Stan, I need you to work this case with me. And I'm worried about you."

"I'll be fine. Not to worry, okay? I'll see you tomorrow."

He clicked off, and I went down the hall to talk to Nick about my phone issue. "Let me do some checking," he said.

I nodded and returned to my desk to check emails and slug down another cup of coffee. Then I headed out the door to Ballet Études. In my experience, repeat visits to a crime scene often turned up some new detail I'd overlooked.

In keeping with my mood, dark clouds hung overhead as I drove to the theater building. No sooner had I parked and stepped out of my car than a heavy rain descended. Naturally, I'd forgotten my umbrella. I dashed to the front door beneath the awning, pressed the bell for admission, and shook myself like a dog on their welcome mat.

Dora, the receptionist with the tie-dyed hair, opened the door and greeted me. "Back again, huh? Looks like you got caught in it," she said.

"Unfortunately." I glanced at the Visitor's Book on her desk. "Do you get many visitors?"

"A fair number. Vendors, folks asking about tickets, donors with big pockets attending open rehearsals, that kind of thing."

"Mind if I take a look at your Visitor's Book?"

She shoved it toward me. "Be my guest."

I scrolled through the names of drop-ins during the weeks prior to Lydia Miseau's death and was surprised to see Sarah Pesetsky's repeated signature. She'd visited seven times in the past two weeks. My antenna shot up.

"This is Victor's ex-wife, isn't it?"

"Yeah. She's like a totally hot shot photographer, you know?"

"No, I didn't know that."

"She's doing a huge project on 'Behind the Scenes in the Arts' for *Connecticut Magazine*. She's done the New Haven Orchestra, the opera company at the Shubert, and now she's doing us—photographing rehearsals, backstage, dressing rooms."

"So, Victor doesn't object to having his ex-wife hanging around?"

She leaned forward and grinned. "Believe me, Victor never lets an opportunity go by for publicity for the company, even if it's courtesy of his ex-wife."

"Got it. How did they seem to get along?"

"From what I heard, it's a case of mutual avoidance. If he sees her coming down the hall, he moves in the other direction, and she turns around and goes the other way."

"And what about Lydia Miseau? Was she bothered by having Victor's ex hanging around?"

"No idea. Lydia was super private about anything personal. She always asked people how they were doing, but avoided talking about herself. Paul Gates might know more. He and Lydia were close."

Paul again. I still wondered about just how close they'd been.

I studied the dates of Sarah Pesetsky's visits one last time. "Doesn't look like she's been here since Lydia passed away."

She shrugged. "She probably got what she needed. And anyway, I doubt she wanted to be around while everyone's grieving for Lydia. A dance company's like a family, you know."

"I see. Thanks." As I slipped inside the theater, the sounds of piano music wafted from above. I climbed the stairs and peeked inside the second-floor main studio. Victor was giving company class. Pairs of dancers crossed the floor on a diagonal doing a series of chaîné turns, followed by a chassé, pas de bourrée, glissade, grand jeté. I was familiar with the lingo from my dance classes as a kid. But the students at my neighborhood dance school had never moved like this. These dancers were gorgeous. Every movement melted seamlessly into the next. The men's leaps hung in the air and took my breath away. I watched for a few minutes and then headed downstairs to poke around.

As I passed the costume shop, I saw a lone figure bent over a sewing machine repairing a tutu. I studied her for a few moments, taking in her straw-like bleached blonde hair and ample figure draped in a long black dress. When she paused, I called out, "Mind if I come in?"

She startled and gasped. "You scared me," she said.

"I'm sorry. I'm Lieutenant O'Connor. Do you have time for a couple of questions?"

She rose and beckoned me in. Her face was deeply lined

and worn, and she looked to be in her forties, maybe early fifties. "Come on in," she said. "Are you the one investigating Lydia's death?"

"I am."

She pulled out a folding chair for me and slid her chair opposite mine. She extended her hand. "I'm Kathy Potter, the wardrobe mistress."

"Pleased to meet you." I pulled out my notebook and scanned the list of folks we'd interviewed that night. "I gather you weren't here last Thursday."

"No, my assistant was covering for me that night. My son got inducted into the National Honor Society at his school, and they had a reception for the inductees and parents."

"You must be proud of him."

"I am." She paused, and her eyes teared up. "I had no idea that when Lydia came in that morning for some last-minute alterations, it would be the last time I'd ever see her."

"Were you close to her?"

"I don't know as how you'd call it close, but I'd known her and worked with her for years. She was a lovely person. Always asked after my son."

"Miss Potter"—

"Please, call me Kathy."

I smiled. "Kathy, did you notice anything different, unusual, going on in the weeks before Lydia died?"

She licked her lips. "Well, she was such a slip of a thing. But I did have to let out the waist on a couple of her costumes. She was almost forty, you know, and I wondered if her body was starting to change a little bit from getting older."

*Or being pregnant.* "Anything else?" I asked.

She paled and looked away. "I'm not sure I should say anything. I mean, she's dead."

"Kathy, this is a suspicious death and possible homicide investigation. I need you to tell me what you know."

She looked around nervously, as though she were checking

to see if anyone else was around. Finally, she said in a low voice, "It must have been a couple of weeks ago. I was supposed to meet Lydia after a production meeting at eleven in the morning. But I got out early and headed down here. I walked in on Lydia and Paul Gates. They were kissing, going at it pretty hot and heavy. I immediately turned around and left. I don't think they saw me. At least I hope not."

"Did it surprise you to see them kissing?"

"Yeah. I knew they were good friends, but Lydia was Victor's wife, and I thought Paul was going with Muriel Gaston. And he's several years younger than Lydia. Not that it was a big deal. Mostly, I guess I was shocked that Lydia looked like, well… like she was romantically involved with someone who wasn't Victor."

I nodded.

She grabbed my arm. "Lieutenant, I'd really appreciate it if you wouldn't say anything to Victor about what I told you. He has enough on his plate right now, and I don't want him to blame me, you know? Shoot the messenger, and all that?"

"Understood." I stood up and gave her my card. "If you think of anything else, give me a call."

———

I headed over to Dr. Stein's office located on the third floor of a rehabbed Victorian in downtown New Haven for my lunchtime therapy appointment. She greeted me warmly and set her watering can down. Her office was covered with a variety of thriving house plants. I always managed to kill mine.

"You must be a gardener," I said.

"I try. Come sit down."

I inhaled the scent of the lit candle on her glass coffee table. She sat across from me, her tortoise-shell glasses perched down her nose. I pegged her as being in her fifties, a tiny frizzy-haired gnome of a woman who could have doubled for Dr. Ruth. Despite her diminutive stature, she radiated strength. And genuine interest. "I'm a candle lover," she said, "but if it bothers you, I'm happy to blow it out."

"No, I love it. Is it lavender?"

"Yes. Supposed to be calming."

"Not sure how helpful that's going to be for me today,"

"I take it your week hasn't gone so well."

"You could say that. Definitely not my favorite." I launched into a description of my frustration at not even being able to tell the cause of death for Lydia Miseau, my worries about Stan, the creepy phone call, and my yo-yo relationship with Chet.

"You have a lot going on. What would you like to focus on?"

I shifted uneasily in my seat. "I guess the Chet thing. I know what I'm doing isn't right. I spend a lot of time beating myself up about it, but I keep seeing him, wanting him. I tell myself I'm going to extricate myself from our relationship, but then I don't."

"Let's backtrack. Last time, you mentioned that he wasn't the first married man you'd been involved with. Tell me about that."

I let out a heavy breath. "In college, I fell for one of my sociology professors. It started when I went to his office to talk with him about one of my criminology papers. He suggested we get some coffee. We ended up talking for hours about his research on serial killers and my dreams of becoming a detective."

"I take it he was older."

"Oh yeah. I was nineteen, and he was thirty-six at the time. I was dazzled. This brilliant guy seemed so interested in talking to me. Pretty soon, we were going for coffee after every class, and he let on about how unhappy he was in his marriage. He said the only reason he didn't divorce his wife was that he couldn't bear to leave his children." I rubbed my chin, thinking about the parallels to Chet's reluctance to lose his kids.

"So, I gather you ended up doing more than coffee together."

Heat worked its way up my neck. "Yes. We started meeting at his office late at night."

"And how did you feel at the time about getting involved with him?"

"It was…a rush. I was flattered. I felt like I mattered, that I was kind of like a savior to him. He seemed so unhappy, and I was someone who could comfort him, be there for him."

"You said that with Chet, you feel guilty and beat yourself up. Were you doing that in college when you were in this relationship?"

I bit the inside of my cheek. "You can't go to Catholic school your whole life and not feel guilty about being a party to adultery. But I kept telling myself I was helping him survive a terrible marriage."

"So how did it end?"

I snorted. "The school year ended, and he took off for Nantucket for the summer with his family. He never wrote or called. I was heartbroken at the time. And that next school year, he took up with another girl. Apparently, that was his pattern."

"Did that make you angry?"

"Disillusioned, mostly. I thought I was a lot more unique, more important to him than it turned out I was."

"When you were involved with him, how would you have felt if he'd told you he was going to leave his wife and wanted to marry you and make a family with you?"

I hesitated. Finally, I said, "I would have been scared, not sure that's what I really wanted."

"Because?"

"I don't know. Selfishly, I wanted to be the desired one, not the ball and chain of the pathetic wife at home."

"So, in your view, a wife is not a desirable role, not one you want to play?"

"I don't know. I mean, my closest friend is happily married and has a career and children. But I have trouble seeing myself ever doing that. Especially now. Being a homicide detective is pretty all-consuming."

"Yes, I can tell it's a demanding job. Were there any other relationships before Chet?"

I bit my lip. "Mostly occasional dates, and a couple of brief affairs with my specialty, married men. Joseph was in training with me at the police academy. We used to study together and, well… one thing led to another. Turned out he hated being a cop. Left the force to go to law school, and we lost touch. And then there was Jeffrey from the public defender's office. I was a witness for the prosecution on a couple of his cases. Despite being on opposing teams, we liked each other. But he wanted to make some real money, so he took a job with some big corporate firm in New York." I shrugged. "Easy come, easy go."

"Doesn't sound like you had the same kind of emotional investment in those relationships the way you had with your professor—and now with Chet."

I sighed. "That's fair to say, I guess. I mean I wasn't in love with those guys—not like I thought I was with my professor— and now with Chet."

She leaned forward. "Okay, so let's talk about what's going on right now with Chet. Do you see any similarities to your college relationship?"

"Unfortunately. There's not the big age difference between Chet and me, so I don't feel the same hero worship I did. But Chet also doesn't want to leave his kids. And I love feeling needed and wanted. And when I'm with him, I don't feel so lonely... But then when I'm not with him, it's all a downward spiral. Sometimes I think I'm going crazy."

"You're very hard on yourself, aren't you?"

Tears burned my eyes. "I'm such a loser."

She gazed at me steadily. "You're not a loser, but from what you've shared with me, you have made a choice, more than once, that has left you feeling badly about yourself. When we continue doing something that leaves us this conflicted, I think it's important to ask ourselves what the payoff is. Whatever the limitations of your relationship with Chet, it's obviously giving you things you cannot bear to give up. And the fact that he is married puts limits on the relationship, which must on some level feel safe to you."

I gulped. "I guess. I haven't really thought about it like that." I rambled for several minutes, not sure at all about my motivations for staying involved with Chet. Clearly, our relationship wasn't going anywhere, and I'd probably be scared shitless if it were.

When our fifty-minute session wrapped up and I rose to go, Dr. Stein said, "I want you to do some more thinking before our next session about all this. What are the payoffs for being involved with someone who is ultimately unavailable for a committed relationship? I want you to ask yourself what you're running toward, as well as what you might be running away from."

I frowned. "I was hoping you could tell me why I keep doing this to myself."

She smiled and shook her head. "Nope. You have to do all the heavy lifting, but I think it's going to be well worth it."

"Let's hope so."

———

By the time I got out of there, my thoughts were swirling, and my stomach was rumbling. I picked up a spicy chicken sandwich from the drive-through and headed back to the office. I stopped in to see Nick to ask about tracing the call I'd gotten the night before.

"Sorry, Caitlin. The phone was purchased for cash at the Wal-Mart on Foxon Boulevard. Then it was used exactly once, to call you, and we traced it to a book return bin at the Fairhaven library branch on Grand Avenue. Wiped clean, of course."

I sighed. "Should have known."

"You should write it up, though. Make a report."

"Will do."

Back at my desk, I filled out a report on my nighttime call, and then I dialed Stan's number.

He picked up on the fifth ring, sounding groggy. "What's up?" he asked.

I filled him in on my talk with Kathy Potter. "Apparently, Paul Gates and Lydia were more than friends."

"Not surprised. Obviously, we need to talk to Paul Gates again."

"Definitely. Now I'm wondering who this baby's daddy was. Oh, and one more thing. Victor's ex-wife, Sarah Pesetsky, was regularly visiting the company in the weeks before Miseau's death. She was working on a project, photographing what goes on behind the scenes."

"Interesting."

"I tell you what, Stan. It's starting to feel like we landed in the middle of a soap opera, and we still don't know if we're dealing with a homicide."

"Yeah, one hot mess. We need to talk to Victor's ex, too… Listen, Cait, I'm really sorry but I'm not sure I'm going to be in tomorrow either. I've been throwing up all day."

I gritted my teeth as anger flushed through me. I wanted to be able to count on Stan, not play nursemaid. "Do what you need to do." I clicked off before I could say something I might regret.

# EIGHT

Muriel dropped by the lighting booth, carrying a double caramel latte, which she handed to Paul.

"What's this?" he asked, surprised to see her. They had avoided one another ever since he'd ended their relationship.

"I remembered this was your favorite. Consider it a peace offering."

"Thanks." He lifted the cup and inhaled the caramel scent. "You remembered." A pang of guilt shot through him. Muriel had always been so thoughtful. And he knew he'd hurt her. A lot.

"I wanted to tell you how sorry I am for your loss. Everyone is so busy comforting Victor, but you were close to Lydia as well."

Paul bit his lip. Was she saying she knew the truth about Lydia and him? He wasn't about to ask. "I appreciate that, Muriel."

"Everyone thinks I must be so happy she's gone." Her voice trembled. "I know people are talking about how I'm gloating because I've inherited all her roles. What they don't understand is I never wanted things to happen like this! I loved Lydia. I still can't believe she's gone."

"Me neither. And I'm sorry about... you know, everything, that went down between us."

"I know. So, I was wondering if you'd ever want to hang out sometime. You know, just as friends?"

Paul closed his eyes for a moment before saying, "I really appreciate your asking, Muriel. But I don't think I'd be particularly good company right now."

She sniffed and picked up her dance bag. "Understood. Just wanted to let you know I'm here for you."

"Means a lot to me. And thanks again for the latte." As he watched her go, Paul couldn't help wondering what would have happened if he'd stayed with Muriel. But there was no point going down that lane. He'd been obsessed with Lydia. Still was.

# NINE

That night, I munched on Chinese take-out and grabbed my trusty legal pad to make notes on my therapy "homework." It was a lot easier to come up with what I was getting out of my love affair. I jotted down, "I love feeling needed, wanted, fawned over." But Melissa had all of that in her marriage to Ronnie. So why did I feel like running for the hills at the thought of a relationship with someone who was actually available? Sure, I could blame it on my dedication to the job, but I knew plenty of cops who bled blue but were also married with kids. I wrote, "FEAR." That felt right. But of what? I sighed. Some detective I was. I couldn't even figure out what spooked me.

I finished the last spring roll, thrust my legal pad aside, and tuned in a Hallmark movie. Much more fun to watch someone else successfully solve her problems and move on to her "Happily Ever After" than dealing with my own messy unresolved issues.

———

No threatening middle-of-the-night phone calls, thank goodness, and I felt immeasurably better the next day. I'd just gotten settled at my desk when my boss, Captain Jameel Singleton, called me into his office for an update.

I sank down in the chair in front of his desk, and he gave me a long look. The captain was famous for his intense dark eyes that didn't miss much. With his shaved head, high cheekbones, and chiseled features, he was what my mom would call a "beautiful man." His looks always made me think of Spenser's Hawk in the Robert B. Parker mystery novels.

Unlike Hawk, however, he spoke in clipped, precise tones. "Where's Stan?"

"He's out sick, sir. Stomach flu."

"Flu, huh? Everything all right with you two? I know he's had a tough time with his wife checking out on him."

I hesitated. Should I say anything about Stan's drinking? What was my responsibility here? No, I didn't want to rat out my partner. "We're okay."

His eyebrows knitted together. "You know you can talk to me if there are issues."

"I do."

"What's the update on the Miseau case?"

I launched into a report about the continuing uncertainty on cause of death and the presence of people close to her who might have had a reason to harm her.

He cracked his knuckles and said, "Stay on it for now, but I can't promise I won't pull you off if we can't establish cause of death."

"Captain, I really hope you'll give me enough time to do that. My gut tells me this was no natural death."

"Unfortunately, I need more than your gut, Lieutenant."

I swallowed hard. "Yes, sir. I understand."

. . .

Back at my desk, I called Chet to check on any updates. There were none, and I cut him off when he whispered that he missed me. "Gotta go," I said abruptly and clicked off.

I called the main number for Ballet Études and got Dora, the receptionist. "Is Paul Gates around?"

"Nah. He's not coming in until this afternoon."

"Okay, I'll try to catch up with him then. Thanks."

With Paul Gates not available until later, I decided to pay a call on Sarah Pesetsky. According to the Motor Vehicle department, she lived outside the city in Bethany, one of the county's wealthiest suburbs. Sure enough, her condo was located in a luxury building on the fourteenth floor. When I buzzed the intercom, a man's slightly shaky voice answered.

"Lieutenant Caitlin O'Connor," I said. "I'm here to speak with Sarah Pesetsky. Is she in?"

"She's in her darkroom, but I'll get her. Come on up." He buzzed me in and greeted me at the door. He looked to be in his eighties and sported a mane of thick white hair and a bushy moustache. "I'm Gerald Gladstone, Sarah's father. Sarah will be out in a minute." Despite the cane, he moved quickly, as he ushered me into the living room. Huge, lush abstract paintings, interspersed with black and white photographs, covered the walls.

"I love your art," I said.

"My late wife owned an art gallery, and I'm a retired art history professor, so over the years, we acquired quite a collection. And of course, Sarah's a marvelous photographer, so we have her work up, too."

"I see that. Very impressive." And it was.

Sarah emerged moments later, wearing a gray smock and silk pants. She had her father's tall, lean build and wore her hair in a carefully arranged frosted bob. Her face was handsome rather than pretty, with nary a wrinkle in sight. I suspected she'd had several Botox treatments. Either that or she'd acquired the services of a skilled plastic surgeon.

Mr. Gladstone excused himself and told his daughter he'd be in the library. Before he left, he said, "Nice to meet you, Lieutenant. Lydia Miseau's death was tragic. Do you know what caused it?"

"Not yet." I glanced at his daughter, who looked like she'd just bitten into something rancid at the mention of Miseau's "tragic" demise. "We're still working on it."

After her father left, Sarah Pesetsky took a seat across from mine. "Lieutenant, what can I do for you?"

"Obviously, I'm investigating the death of Ms. Miseau, and I have a few questions for you."

"I can't imagine how I could help, but what did you want to ask me?"

"I understand you were working on a photography project and had spent quite a bit of time at Ballet Études in the weeks before Ms. Miseau passed away."

"That's true."

"Did you notice anything unusual or suspicious on your shoots?"

"No. Nothing. The company was getting ready for the opening of *Romeo and Juliet*, so things were hectic, but that's not unusual."

"Was it at all uncomfortable for you to spend time with your ex-husband or with Ms. Miseau?"

She snorted. "We spent extraordinarily little time together, actually. Victor and I have become quite good at avoiding one another, and as I'm sure you can understand, things were awkward between Lydia and me."

"But obviously, you must have wanted to include her in your project."

"It was no problem. I photographed her dressing room when she wasn't around and stationed myself in the wings when I shot photos of her rehearsing on stage."

"I see. Do you know if she had any enemies, anyone who might have wanted to harm her?"

She shrugged. "I have no idea. Needless to say, we didn't have a close personal relationship."

"Were you aware she was six weeks pregnant when she died?"

Her eyes widened. Then she laughed. "That must have been quite a shock for poor old Victor."

"What do you mean?"

"Victor had a vasectomy years ago before we split up. Actually, we had quite a row about it. I wanted more children, and he did not. Sad to say, the man only likes his children once they're not children anymore."

"Sometimes the procedure can be reversed."

"Trust me. Victor's the last person who'd ever be interested in having another child."

"Interesting. Anything else you'd like to tell me?"

"No. I'm sorry that this interview has provided me with more interesting information than it's given you. What's that expression? 'What goes around comes around'? Victor's not only lost his child bride, but she was catting about on him. I call that divine justice."

She sounded so bitter. And pleased.

"Well, if you think of anything else, please give me a call," I said and handed her my card.

"That's very doubtful, Lieutenant, but I'm delighted you came to see me."

After I left, it occurred to me Frederick hadn't told his mother about Lydia Miseau's pregnancy. I wondered why. Weren't they close? Or was Lydia Miseau a subject he preferred not to discuss with his mother? I'd certainly noticed his mother's pleasure in learning Miseau had apparently been unfaithful to her ex-husband.

I ordered my usual chicken salad sandwich to go at Marco's and headed over to Ballet Études to see if I could catch the very "close friend" of the deceased. "Hey Dora," I said when I entered the lobby. "Has Paul Gates come in?"

"He's here."

"Great." I entered the theater and the sounds of a class in progress wafted overhead. I was tempted to go up and watch, but I really wanted to talk to Gates. I checked the lighting booth, but he wasn't there. Then I walked through the stage and backstage area and still didn't find him. Finally, I went downstairs and peered into the costume shop and the dressing rooms. Nothing.

I paused at Lydia's closed dressing room, cordoned off with crime scene tape. On a hunch, I pushed the door open, ducked under the tape, and flicked on the light. Paul Gates sat hunched over in the makeup chair, his head in his hands. He raised his tear-filled eyes to me.

"What are you doing here? This area is off limits."

"I'm sorry," he said, his voice catching. "I just wanted to feel close to Lydia. Can you smell her scent? Lilacs—she couldn't get enough of them."

"You really can't be in here. Did you touch anything?"

"No!"

"You weren't telling me the truth, were you? You and Lydia were more than friends."

"She's gone now. What does it matter? Let Victor bury his wife in peace."

"It matters because her death is suspicious, a possible homicide. And if it is homicide, she deserves justice. I need you to tell me the truth."

"All right, all right. Lydia and I were lovers."

"And the baby?"

"Ours."

"Did Victor know?"

He rubbed his temples. "I don't know. He hasn't directly accused me, but he probably suspects."

"What were you planning to do?"

"I wanted her to leave Victor, be with me, raise our child together. I'd get another job. We'd start over."

"And she agreed?"

"At first. And then a week before she died, she said she couldn't do it. She thought Victor would punish us, blackball me, and was sure we'd starve. She was so frightened. She told me she was going to ask for his forgiveness and stay in the marriage. She'd offer to serve as his rehearsal coach, teach in the school, continue to be useful to him."

There was that word again. Useful. "And the baby?"

"It would be raised as Victor's and her child. No one would know."

"But you knew. How did you feel about her change of heart?"

"I begged her. I cried. I ranted. But she was adamant."

"But you could have fought this—appealed to the court, filed a paternity test."

"I loved her, Lieutenant. I couldn't do that to Lydia. And I need to work. I'd already told Victor I was leaving at the end of the season. If I had any prayer of him not blackballing me, I had to stay silent, let her go. Let my child go." He wiped away a stray tear.

"This must have made you angry at Lydia for rejecting you, and announcing she planned to raise your child as Victor's."

"I would never harm Lydia if that's what you're implying. But I'm human. There have been days when I felt like I was being eaten alive by my own anger, and other times when the weight of my sadness made me question whether I could even go on. But thankfully, my bleakest moments recede. And what remains is my love for her. And my memories."

"Do you have any idea what killed her?"

He shook his head. "No. She was so strong, so vibrant."

"And do you suspect anyone of harming her?"

"I don't know. Victor obviously had reasons to be upset with her, but the man is ultimately a pragmatist. Even in retirement, Lydia was more valuable to him alive than dead.

She wasn't only a brilliant dancer, but she was a remarkable coach and mentor to younger dancers."

"And if he didn't see it that way? Do you think he is capable of murder?"

His jaw dropped. "To be perfectly honest, Lieutenant, I have no idea. Who can say what anyone else is capable of?"

"Fair point. Anything else you want to tell me?"

He shook his head.

"All right. You need to leave this area. Now."

He nodded and slipped under the crime tape and out the door. After he left, I looked around Lydia's dressing room—the gorgeous costumes, pointe shoes, makeup, and a sad looking bouquet of wilted flowers. I bit my lip. What—and who—killed Lydia?

# TEN

On my way out, I ran into Gus, the custodian, sweeping the hallway. His bald head glistened with sweat. I wondered if he'd overheard any of my conversation with Paul Gates. Probably not.

"How are you doing?" I asked.

"Can't complain. Doesn't feel the same around here without Ms. Miseau."

"How is your wife?" I remembered how much it meant to him that Lydia Miseau had always asked about her.

His shoulders sagged. "Not so good. Her cancer's bad. Say a prayer for us, okay?"

I touched his arm. "I will. I'm so sorry to hear that."

"Rough year." He turned away to continue his sweeping.

"Say Gus, I guess you regularly clean down here, don't you?"

"Sure."

"Can you tell me who frequently came into Ms. Miseau's dressing room?"

He squinted at me. "Let me think… Mr. Pesetsky came in a lot. Sometimes Muriel Gaston would stop by, ask her for dancing advice. Ms. Miseau was kind of like her teacher. And

59

umm, Kathy, you know, the one that does the costumes—she was in and out. And Paul Gates. He and Ms. Miseau hung out a lot." He paused and his eyes darted around as though he were checking to see if anyone could hear us.

Was it my imagination, or did he seem suddenly nervous? "Anyone else?" I asked.

"Well, Sarah Pesetsky came by a few times to photograph all the dressing rooms, including Ms. Miseau's, for that project she was working on."

"Okay. Do you recall Frederick Pesetsky ever coming by?"

He shook his head. "No, but that doesn't mean he didn't. I'm in charge of cleaning the whole building, and I'm not always down here."

"Understood." I handed him a card. "If you think of anything else, can you give me a call?"

"Sure thing, Lieutenant. Do you know what killed Ms. Miseau?"

God, I was sick of people asking me that. "Not yet, but we're working on it."

———

By the time I returned to the station, I was bushed. I put in a call to Stan to update him. He still sounded groggy, but he was coherent.

"So, guess who had a vasectomy?"

"You're kidding—the husband of the dead ballerina?"

"Bingo."

"How'd you find that out?"

"I interviewed his ex-wife today. She seemed thrilled that Lydia, the replacement wife, was apparently running around on Victor. Don't think there's much love lost there."

"Huh... So who's the baby's daddy-- Gates?"

"You've got it. He admitted it to me today. But Miseau had

broken things off with him. She decided to stick it out with Victor and raise the baby as theirs."

"Weirder and weirder. You can't make this crap up."

"True. So, we've got Victor whose wife was having an affair, Paul, the rejected lover, and Muriel, the understudy who was dumped by Paul. Meantime, the ex-wife is hanging around photographing the company and wasn't fond of her replacement. Oh, and we might as well throw in Frederick, who had reason to dislike Miseau and no doubt is excited about getting the company out of financial trouble, thanks to the insurance money."

He snorted. "Caitlin, they all sound possible. But we've got to figure out how she was killed."

"I know. Captain Singleton warned me today if we don't figure that out soon, he's pulling us off the case."

"Well, shit."

"Shit is right. Please tell me you're coming back tomorrow. We need to talk to Pesetsky again—see what he says about that little vasectomy issue. And I want to talk to Muriel Gaston again."

"I'll be there."

———

When I got home that night, I found a message from Melissa on my landline. "Come to dinner with us on Saturday, okay? We're celebrating the beginning of spring break, and we're leaving the next day for Disney World. I want to see you before we go. We were thinking Skappo's around seven? Let me know."

I called back and told her dinner sounded great. I wanted a night away from thinking about the case. And Chet.

I poured myself a glass of wine and heated up the last of my Chinese take-out. Then I tuned in the news, but my mind kept wandering back to Lydia Miseau. The more I learned about the ballerina's complicated relationships, the more convinced I was someone close to her had killed her. But how?

What about what she was wearing? Her costume must be in the evidence room—the long white nightgown, tights, her pointe shoes. Suppose there was something on one of them that had caused her heart to shut down? Was that even possible? When nothing had shown up in the tests thus far?

It wouldn't hurt to ask. Even though I was trying not to keep tempting myself, I wanted to talk to Chet face to face about possibilities. I decided to pay a visit to him the next day.

# ELEVEN

While Caitlin watched the news that night, Gus Mikowski, Ballet Études' chief custodian, was across town in the modest one-bedroom flat he shared with his wife, Mary.

She was so painfully thin and coaxing her to eat anything was getting harder and harder.

"Please, Sweetheart," he said. "I fixed your favorite, chicken noodle casserole. Try to take a few bites, won't you? You've got to keep up your strength."

"I'm trying, Gus." She reluctantly took a bite, then put her fork down. "I just have no appetite."

"Two more bites? Please? For me?"

"I'll try. One more." She picked up her fork and took a tiny bite.

"Tell me what Doctor Scorvino said today."

"Oh Gus, are you sure you want to hear this? It's not good."

"Of course, I do. Tell me."

"He says the tumor hasn't responded the way they'd hoped. There's only one more treatment they can try—it's still experimental, but insurance won't cover it. Honey, I think the time has come to call in hospice. I want to stay home with you, be with you, when the end comes."

Gus's eyes filled with tears, and he flung his napkin down. "No way. We're not giving up yet. Tell the doctor we want to try the treatment."

"With what money? We've spent every dime we have. I don't want to leave you totally bankrupt. That's not fair to you."

"Mary, you're my whole world. Nothing else matters. I promise you I will find the money to pay for the treatment, you hear me? You call the doctor tomorrow and tell him we want to move on this."

"Are you sure?"

"Absolutely. Have I ever let you down?"

She smiled wanly at him. "Never."

# TWELVE

Stan came in on time the next morning. I was so glad to have him back, but he looked terrible. His droopy eyes were bloodshot, and his skin had taken on a grayish pallor.

"You okay?" I asked.

"I'm here. What's on the docket?"

I told him about my idea that maybe the ballerina had come into contact with something that led to her heart shutting down.

"I don't know, Cait. That sounds a little 'out there.'"

I shrugged. "I thought I'd at least talk to Chet about it."

"At this point, anything is worth a shot. You still want to talk to Pesetsky again?"

"Yup. You ready to rock and roll?"

"Only if coffee's involved."

"We'll make a pit stop first."

---

We found the artistic director in his office. He was wearing his rehearsal clothes—gray sweatpants, a T-shirt with the Ballet Études logo on the front, and soft-soled black shoes.

He did not look happy to see us, especially when I told him we had more questions.

"Detectives, I'm getting ready to teach company class." He looked at his watch. "I can only give you a few minutes."

I went direct. "That's fine, sir. Is it true you've had a vasectomy, and the baby your late wife was expecting was apparently not yours?"

He let out a heavy breath. "I suppose you've been talking to my charming ex-wife."

I didn't respond.

"Can't we let Lydia rest in peace? This is a horrible invasion of our privacy and totally unnecessary."

"Mr. Pesetsky, with all due respect, your wife died under suspicious circumstances," I said. "It's our responsibility to investigate, and that includes learning all we can about her close relationships."

He sighed. "What do you want to know?"

"How did you really feel about your wife's pregnancy and her apparent infidelity?"

He sank back in his seat, and his shoulders sagged. "I wasn't thrilled. But Lydia begged my forgiveness, insisted she wanted to stay in the marriage, and raise this child as ours."

"And you agreed to that?" Stan asked.

"I did, on the condition that after her retirement, she would continue to serve as our rehearsal coach and mentor our up-and-coming dancers. And of course, I insisted my name would go on the birth certificate and the man she'd slept with would sign a non-disclosure agreement. I wanted him out of our lives, and I certainly didn't want him to have anything to do with the child."

I leaned forward. "Did you know the identity of her lover?"

"I'm not stupid, Lieutenant. Gates has assured me he's leaving at the end of the season and had he not resigned, rest assured I would have demanded it."

I pressed on. "You gave up your first marriage and left your family to marry Lydia Miseau. This must have felt like quite a betrayal. You've told us she begged your forgiveness. Did you, in fact, forgive her?"

"Ha. Good one. The most honest answer I can give you is that I was working on it. I worshiped my wife, Lieutenant. She was truly magical, the most beautiful, inspiring dancer I've ever worked with. And she had the unusual ability to pass it on. I can't begin to tell you the marvelous things she brought out in Muriel's dancing. Truthfully, I needed her for my work, for the company."

"Did you harm your wife, Mr. Pesetsky? She not only betrayed you, but the insurance money would have rescued the company from serious financial trouble."

His face reddened, and he stood up. "What did I just tell you? Of course not. Lydia had talents that were worth much more to me than money. Now, I really must go and teach class."

After he stalked out, I turned to Stan. "As far as I can tell, he carries a calculator around to measure everyone's value according to what they can do for his ballet company. He's telling us she was worth more to him alive than dead. Do you believe him?"

"Don't know," Stan said. "But I don't think it could have been any picnic to be married to him. You know how I feel about women who cheat. But in this case? I can see why Lydia Miseau had her reasons."

"And yet, she didn't leave."

"Yeah. Makes you wonder."

"She was afraid, I think. And we don't make the best decisions when we're frightened."

Stan lifted his eyebrows and gave me a long look. But he didn't say anything.

I was almost positive he wanted to say something about my relationship with Chet. Once again, when I thought about my reluctance to pull the plug, the word "fear" flashed across my mind in neon lights. What was I so afraid of?

# THIRTEEN

On our way out, we passed the costume shop. Kathy Potter stood in the doorway and motioned us inside. She shut the door behind us.

"I... I thought of something else about that morning, you know, before Lydia passed away." She clasped her hands tightly against her chest. "I don't want to get anyone in trouble, you know? But I decided I'd better tell you."

"Go ahead, Kathy. It's okay," I said, trying to sound reassuring.

"Well, I was coming out of Lydia's dressing room. I'd dropped off a costume I'd repaired when Frederick brushed by me. I told him she wasn't there, and he said, 'Oh, it's okay. I'll wait for her. She should be on her way down from rehearsal any minute.' I thought it was odd, because... well, she and Frederick weren't that friendly. It was no secret he resented her for breaking up his parents' marriage."

"Had you ever seen him visiting her in her dressing room before?" Stan asked.

She shook her head. "No, never. Like I said, there was no love lost there. Look, you don't have to tell anyone where you heard this from, do you?"

I touched her arm. "We'll do our best not to mention your name, but you have to understand we're investigating a suspicious death."

She heaved a heavy sigh. "I guess I feel better getting this off my chest."

"We really appreciate your honesty," I told her. "Call me if you think of anything else."

———

We walked down the hall. "You thinking what I'm thinking?" Stan asked.

"Yup. This fits with what Gus told us. He'd never seen Frederick drop in on Lydia. No time like the present. Let's go talk to him."

His door was ajar when we knocked on the frame. His eyebrows shot up when he saw us and motioned us in. Sheets of what looked like expense reports were spread all over his desk.

"What brings you back to see me, Detectives?"

"We're wondering what you were doing in Lydia Miseau's dressing room the morning she died," I said.

His eyes widened. He hesitated, then said, "You've been talking to Kathy Potter, I suppose?"

I didn't answer his question, but asked one of my own. "It's my understanding you kept your distance from Ms. Miseau and weren't in the habit of dropping in on her. What were you doing there?"

He gestured to the papers on his desk. "See these? Take a look. We're drowning in debt. I had an idea Lydia could help us charm our patrons into opening their pocketbooks a bit wider."

"How could she do that?" I asked.

"She was an expert schmoozer. I wanted to pitch the idea to

her of inaugurating a series of 'Lunches with Lydia' where donors would feel they were getting extra special treatment, spending time up close and personal with the company's star."

"Did she think it was a good idea?"

He pressed his fingers into his temple and shook his head. "I'll never know. I'd seen Victor come downstairs after reviewing a couple of changes he wanted to make in her last scene with Alexander. I expected her to come down to her dressing room, and I waited for several minutes. But she never showed. I figured she'd gotten caught up in talking to one of the dancers or... maybe Gates." He curled his nose at the mention of Gates' name. "I didn't stick around to ask, decided to catch her after the dress rehearsal. By then, it was obviously too late."

"Did you mention your idea of 'Lunches with Lydia' to anyone else?"

"I told my father I had a new fundraising idea, but I didn't go into any details. He's pretty distracted right before an opening."

"Did you notice anyone else near her dressing room that morning?"

"Only Kathy Potter. She does a wonderful job as our wardrobe mistress, but she's a huge gossip. And trust me when I say she doesn't always have her facts right."

———

As Stan and I walked back to the car, he said, "What did you think of his explanation?"

"Plausible. He's telling the truth about the company's financial situation. But about what he was doing in her dressing room? No idea. We can't count him out. He didn't like her and that insurance money sure would have helped pull the company out of its financial morass."

"No kidding. That stuff everyone told us about Lydia being beloved by all? Not true when it came to Frederick."

———

Back in the office, we did some paperwork and went out to an early lunch together at Wendy's. I was partial to their spicy chicken sandwiches, and Stan always let me share his fries.

He declined to go with me for my drop-in on Chet, and I was glad he didn't come. I arrived just in time to see Chet returning from what must have been a cozy lunch with his adorably petite and oh-so-blonde wife, Marian. The two were walking down the hall, chatting, and laughing, their arms entwined. So much for how miserable he was in his marriage. What a liar!

I was several yards behind them in the hallway. I thought about turning around and leaving, but I really wanted to talk to Chet about Miseau's cause of death.

They both entered the office, and I tapped on the door frame seconds later. "So sorry to interrupt," I said. "I have a few questions for you, Chet, about the Miseau case."

He looked startled to see me, but made a quick recovery. "Of course, Lieutenant. You've met my wife, Marian, haven't you?"

"I have. Nice to see you again."

She extended her hand to me which was ice cold. "You, too," she said, her cool tone matching the temperature of her hand. She turned to her husband. "I'm off to pick up the kids, darling. Don't forget we've got that dinner tonight with the Goldrings." She made a big show of kissing him goodbye. On the lips. Was she marking her territory for my benefit? Did she suspect anything? Hard to tell.

After she left, neither of us said anything for a moment. Finally, he said, "Sorry about that. I know what you're thinking."

"No, I don't think you do."

"It's not what you think, Cait. I've gotten pretty good at pretending everything's a-okay when I'm with Marian."

"Didn't look like an act to me, Chet. Believe me, I get it."

He stood up and moved toward me. "You don't understand. It's not what it looks like. I can't even sleep because I'm always thinking about you."

I held my hand up. I didn't want to touch him. Or have him touch me. "I've heard great things about *Ambien* for sleeplessness. But what I came to see you about was a question I have."

He sighed and retreated back to his chair. "What is it?"

"Was there anything Lydia Miseau could have come in contact with that could have caused her heart to shut down but wouldn't necessarily be detectable—like maybe even something on her costumes?"

Chet rubbed his chin. "Huh—hadn't thought of that, but it's possible. If her skin absorbed something, for instance, blood pressure medication, it wouldn't have killed her immediately, but it eventually would have slowed her heart to the point where it simply stopped. And the medication flushes through the system pretty fast."

My mind shot back to Stan's and my first interview with Victor, when he suddenly went for his heart medication. "What about nitroglycerin?"

"Same deal."

"Okay then. I'm going to arrange to have all her costumes checked and her warmup clothes as well. Who knows? Maybe we'll get lucky."

Back in the office, I told Stan all about my meeting with Chet—minus the gory details about running into his wife and witnessing their lovey-dovey relationship.

"This could be it," Stan said. "You're a genius."

"Hardly. But it sure would be nice to catch a break on this." I filled out the paperwork and made a bunch of phone calls to get the ball rolling on testing Miseau's costumes. After that, we went to Captain's weekly staff meeting.

As we were leaving the precinct for the day, I got a surprise phone call from Victor Pesetsky inviting Stan and me to the opening performance of *Romeo and Juliet* the next night. "I am very pleased with the company's work, given this terrible tragedy. Muriel is doing well, taking on such a huge responsibility dancing the role of Juliet, and it's in large part because of the wonderful coaching she received from Lydia."

He sounded positively buoyant, hardly like any grieving widower I'd ever met. "Thank you for the invitation. I don't know if Stan's available, but yes, I'll be there."

Stan rolled his eyes when I told him about the invite. "You go without me, Cait. Ballet is not my thing, and besides, I have other plans."

Knowing Stan, "other plans" amounted to drinking himself into oblivion. As we walked out to the parking lot, I tried to tell myself Stan's drinking wasn't my problem. Except it really was.

———

That night, I had an anxiety dream. Despite my protests, Victor Pesetsky was pushing me onstage and telling me to take over dancing the role of Juliet. "But I don't know the steps," I kept trying to explain, "and I'm a terrible dancer." When my phone rang, I startled awake, relieved at the cancellation of my dancing debut.

But my relief was short-lived. When I picked up, the same distorted voice said, "Do the world a favor and die, bitch, die."

Hot anger tore through me. "Listen, you cowardly creep, you're taking your life in your hands, harassing a cop."

The only response was a click as my friendly caller disconnected.

Who the hell was doing this? And why? Who had reason to hate me who wasn't currently locked up?

But maybe this wasn't work-related. What about Chet's wife, Marian? She sure hadn't been overly friendly. Had she figured out Chet and I were involved and decided to scare me off? It occurred to me that the first call came the day after Chet had hammered on my door and ended up spending the night. Coincidence? My dad, a former police chief, used to say coincidences rarely existed. They alerted an investigator to something "smelly and suspicious."

Still, it was hard to imagine Chet's suburban wife shopping for the necessary equipment to pull this off, not to mention getting up in the middle of the night to harass me. But what did I know?

Not much. I pounded the pillow and plopped back down on my bed, determined to go back to sleep.

Unfortunately, determination can be highly overrated.

———

The next morning, I considered talking to Captain Singleton about the threatening phone calls, but decided against it. I didn't want to get anywhere near the question of who might have a reason to go after me in my personal life. So, I filed another report, complained to Stan, and generally felt sorry for myself. I ended up spending most of the day helping Vince, our department's newest and greenest detective, interview witnesses in a fatal robbery shooting. At least I managed to sneak in a nap before heading to the opening of *Romeo and Juliet*.

It was nice being at the ballet when I wasn't on duty intent on tracking down witnesses and possible suspects. I could appreciate the company's intimate performing space. The theater seated around 800, and its ornate early twentieth century décor thrust me into another world. The domed high ceiling featured a mural of dancing nymphs and angels. Enormous crystal chandeliers hung from above.

Tonight, the place was packed. A hushed silence descended upon the audience as Victor came out before the performance and explained that the company was dedicating the production to "the memory of my beloved wife, the incomparable ballerina, Lydia Miseau." He went on to say that Lydia had worked closely with Muriel Gaston, and he was gratified the audience members could witness her debut as Juliet.

I thought Gaston danced with youthful energy and innocence and imagined that Lydia Miseau would have been pleased. The balcony scene was especially moving, as were the scenes between Juliet and her faithful nursemaid. And thankfully, Muriel did not miss her cue to awaken in Act III.

Afterward, she and Alexander and the rest of the dancers received several curtain calls, and Gaston was showered with flowers. Victor Pesetsky joined them on stage for a final bow and appeared delighted with the successful opening night. Once again, I was struck by his ebullient demeanor. He did not look like a man who had lost his wife little more than a week ago.

# FOURTEEN

A light rain fell Saturday night as I drove to dinner at Skappo's. When I arrived, Melissa and Ronnie were already settled at their table. As I crossed the cozy restaurant, I realized they were not alone. An attractive man with black curly hair, a moustache, and wire-rimmed glasses was sitting with them. Hmmm… was this a setup? Melissa knew how I hated fixups. But then again, she was one determined friend.

Best to be gracious. I pasted a smile on my face and greeted everyone.

"There you are," Melissa said. "I want you to meet one of my good friends from school, Hank Miller."

He stood up, and I noticed that he was tall, well over six feet, and he had a wonderfully warm and wide smile. He moved to hold my chair out for me, and I thanked him. I considered myself a feminist, but I was still a fan of old-time etiquette.

My gaze automatically went to his left hand. No sign of a wedding ring. "It's nice to meet you," I said. "Are you a teacher, too?"

"Sure am. My classroom's two doors down from Melissa's.

I teach science and coach the basketball team." His voice was so deep. And resonant. An unexpected flash of lightness crossed my chest.

Melissa broke in then. "Cait, you're always telling me I'm the only one you know who loves teaching middle schoolers. Well, Hank does as well. Last year, he won our district's 'Teacher of the Year.'"

He looked faintly embarrassed at Melissa's obvious effort to impress me with his datable credentials. "It's all true," he admitted.

"What do you like about teaching middle schoolers?" I asked.

"They're funny and eager and curious about everything. But they're also having a hard time with so much developmental change. They're certain that everyone in the world is watching them and judging them. I feel like whatever we trusted adults can do to ease their transition into adolescence is good."

"You're right about imagining everyone is looking at you at that age. I remember feeling so awkward and self-conscious. Thirteen was definitely the worst."

The waiter appeared and, after consulting with us, Ronnie ordered a bottle of their house red wine.

Hank turned to me. "Melissa tells me you're a homicide detective. That must be challenging work."

"It is. But like you, I'm pretty passionate about my job. My late father was in law enforcement, and I grew up thinking that catching bad guys was the world's coolest job. I think it's a calling, probably a lot like you feel about teaching."

He leaned toward me. "Exactly. The pay's not the greatest, the hours are long, but I wouldn't trade what I do for a living."

He had the warmest brown eyes. They crinkled around the edges when he grinned. I couldn't help smiling back.

The waiter arrived with our wine, and Ronnie insisted Melissa be the official taster. She pronounced it "excellent," and after all our glasses were filled, Ronnie proposed a toast "To friendships, old and new."

We pored over the menu and decided to share two orders of the antipasti dish, *Salsa Tartufata*, an Italian truffle, and mushroom spread on toasted ciabatta bread with fresh mozzarella. Conversation flowed easily, as Melissa and Hank told funny stories about their students. "There's absolutely no direct communication when it comes to romance," Melissa said. "If Crystal has a crush on Roberto, she tells her girlfriend Annie who consults with Roberto's friend Carlos to find out if Roberto might be interested."

"I remember that," I said. "It's way too scary to speak directly to someone you have a crush on." I turned to Hank. "Do you have any grunters? My older brothers used to drive my parents crazy when they got into middle school. They responded to everything my mom and dad asked by grunting or giving a one syllable answer. A question like, 'What was the best thing that happened to you today?' would be followed by some noncommittal response, like, 'Nothin.' It drove my parents wild."

"I think that's more of a parent-child problem," Hank said. "At school, our issue is getting them to stop talking."

Ronnie got into the act by describing his middle school woes when he was trying to impress Glenda Morrell, the hottest girl in seventh grade, with his "come hither" look and accidentally walked into a telephone pole at the bus stop.

The food arrived, and we dug in. The antipasti was scrumptious. By the time our entrées arrived, I was well on my way to being full. My *Spaghetti alla Carbonara* was delicious but very heavy. "I may never eat again," I said, when I finally had to push my plate away. Of course, when Melissa suggested we share a chocolate mousse with crushed almonds and fresh whipped cream, I didn't say no.

We lingered over coffee and dessert, and I couldn't help noticing how Hank's gaze kept finding mine. And he asked me lots of questions about my work and life. My stomach fluttered. I was pretty sure it wasn't from overeating.

Melissa asked him how Jack was doing.

"He's great. I love being with him."

Oh no. Had I gotten all the signals wrong? Was someone named Jack his partner?

He must have noticed my confused expression, because he said, "Jack's my little boy. He's seven. My ex-wife and I share custody."

"Great age," I said. "Is it hard to co-parent with your ex?" I hoped I wasn't being too intrusive. Must be the detective in me asking him something so personal.

He didn't seem fazed by my question. "Sometimes. But he really needs both of us in his life, and we try hard to keep things friendly. We make it a rule to never say anything negative about one another to him."

"You know, I think that was the hardest thing about my parents splitting up," Melissa said. "Mom was so angry about my father leaving her for another woman, and she constantly complained about him. It was awful. Remember, Cait?"

I put my hand over hers. "I do. I felt so bad for you."

Ronnie put his arm around his wife. "The good news is you'll never have that problem in our marriage. You are so stuck with me."

Melissa fake-fanned herself. "I'll bear up somehow." She winked at her husband and then gave him a quick kiss on the cheek.

They were so good together. I wondered if I could ever have something like their marriage. Was I capable? Did I even want that? I wasn't sure, and the frustrating thing was I didn't know why I was so damned ambivalent.

As we were leaving, Hank turned to me and said in a low voice, "May I call you sometime?"

"That'd be nice." I gave him my number. Feeling suddenly shy, I slipped out the door ahead of him. For the first time since I'd gotten involved with Chet, I felt the glimmers of attraction for another man. But was it fair to start something I couldn't deliver on? I wasn't in the business of hurting other people. Or maybe I was. A picture of Chet's wife and their children flashed across my mind. I tried to push away the image, but the darned thing hung around, anyway.

# FIFTEEN

Stan looked worse to me Monday morning. Huge bags hung beneath his red-rimmed eyes, and his nose was starting to take on a bulbous look, with bluish veins threading their way through it.

"Bad weekend?" I asked.

"Not great, but hey, I'm here. How about you? Any more phone calls from your creeper?"

"Thank God, no." I thought about telling Stan about meeting Hank, but I wasn't ready to go there. "You up for going to Ballet Études and talking to Muriel Gaston again?"

"Sure. How was the opening, by the way?"

"Big success. Victor dedicated the performance to his late wife, and Muriel danced well. I figure she must be thrilled to finally have what she's been in line for. And Victor was soaking it all up. I've never seen anyone look less like a grieving widower."

"Makes you wonder, doesn't it?"

"No kidding."

"When are the tests supposed to come back on the costumes?"

"Not for several days."

We walked to the car, and I inhaled the scent of newly blooming hyacinths. I loved this time of year. We grabbed two coffees on the way and rode with the windows down.

Dora greeted us in the lobby. Today, her hair was bright orange and looked newly permed. "You two back again?"

"Yes, ma'am," I said. "Is Muriel Gaston around?"

"Oh yeah. She's here. Company's got the day off, but a writer from *Seasons Arts and Culture* is interviewing her for a feature story." She looked at her watch. "They should be finishing up pretty soon. They're in the Green Room."

"Thanks," I said.

We headed inside and found Muriel shaking hands with a guy who looked the part of an arts writer—beard, ponytail, and tweed sports jacket over jeans.

When she spotted us, her smile faltered. She returned her attention to the writer. "Looking forward to your article, Eric. Thanks so much."

He nodded to us as we passed him on our way toward Muriel. As we drew closer, she repeated Dora's line. "Back again?"

"We have a few more questions," I said.

She gestured for us to come in. The smell of stale coffee hit me as we took seats around the ancient oak coffee table in the corner. My armchair was grayish blue, lumpy and threadbare. I gathered outfitting the Green Room was low priority for the cash-strapped company.

"I came to your opening night," I told her. "You danced beautifully. Saw the lovely review in Sunday's paper. You must be very pleased."

"I am." She smiled, then added, "Of course, with Lydia's passing, it's bittersweet. As I told you, she was my mentor."

"How did you feel about your former boyfriend, Paul Gates, breaking things off with you and then becoming involved with her?"

She stiffened. "You're obviously very thorough, Lieutenant.

I was hurt, if you must know. I don't think anybody enjoys being dumped, do you?"

Stan nodded vigorously, his own experience ever-present in his thinking. "That must have been tough on you losing your man to the same person who stood between you and the chance to dance roles you'd waited for years to take on."

Her enormous blue eyes narrowed. "As I told you before, I knew my time would come. And Lydia was helping me prepare. I owe a great deal to her."

"Did her involvement with Gates create tension between the two of you?" I asked.

She drew herself up and turned her steely gaze on me. "We never discussed it. I'm sure Lydia hoped I didn't know about their relationship, but I'm not stupid. It was obvious."

"Regardless of whether the two of you discussed it, did this make you angry or resentful toward her?"

She held her hands up. "What do you want me to say? Did I like being thrown over by my boyfriend of three years for the company star? No. Did I like waiting year after year for Lydia to decide to retire? No. Did I harm her? Absolutely not."

"Do you have any idea who might have harmed her?"

"No. Everyone loved Lydia. Personally, I think she probably died from some freak natural cause, and you're beating a dead horse. Have you figured out what killed her?"

I shook my head. "We're still working on it."

"Well, good luck with that." She stood up. "If there's nothing else, I have an appointment for a massage."

"Okay. Thanks," I said, and we watched her strut off, her gorgeous feet turned out in typical duck-like dancer fashion.

On the way out, we ran into Frederick Pesetsky who was just coming in. He carried a large leather briefcase. The lines etched across his forehead appeared deeper than I remembered. "Any news, Detectives?"

"Nothing definitive," I said. "But congratulations on your successful opening."

"Thank you, but frankly, I'm concerned about all this delay. We're unable to collect on the insurance without a death certificate that indicates Lydia died of natural causes. Surely you can understand we'd like to get the investigation resolved."

"I can. As soon as we've wrapped things up, we'll contact you immediately."

"I'll count on that. Good day, detectives." He nodded to Dora and swept past us.

"Have you noticed everyone associated with the company excels at making dramatic exits?" I asked Stan.

He laughed. "It's very effective. We should take notes."

Back in the car, I said, "So. What did you think?"

"Starting to feel like we're spinning our wheels. A bunch of people close to Lydia had reasons to be angry at her. Regardless of what she claims, that includes Muriel Gaston. And even Victor's son Frederick, who's dying to collect the insurance money. Not to mention Victor's ex who was hanging around taking pictures those last weeks. But until we figure out cause of death, we're stuck in neutral, you know?"

"The ex seems doubtful," Stan said. "They've been divorced forever."

"I wouldn't be so sure. My best friend's mom still has fantasies of revenge toward her dad, and he left decades ago."

"Hmmm." Stan pulled out a small thermos from his jacket pocket and took a swig.

"If that's coffee, can I have a sip?"

"It's not. Don't think you'd like it."

The scent of beer wafted in my direction. My mouth gaped open. "Geez, Stan. What the hell do you think you're doing? Drinking on the job? Have you lost your mind?"

He jammed the lid closed and thrust the thermos back into his pocket. "Sorry. Sometimes I feel like a tiny nip will help me get through the day. I've been so jittery lately."

Frustration gnawed at me. I stared at him in the heavy

silence. Finally, I said, "Stan, you're my partner and my friend. I care about you. But you're out of control. Either you stop drinking and go to A.A., or I'll be forced to tell Captain Single-ton. You're endangering yourself—and me as your partner."

He wagged his finger at me. "Tell you what, Caitlin. You report me to the Captain, and I'll be forced to fill him in on your little extra-curricular romance with dear old Chet, our very married medical examiner. Don't think that's copasetic in our departmental rule book either."

My skin prickled. "You're threatening me because I want you to get help?"

"I'm just sayin'. If I'm out of control, which, by the way, I'm not, so are you."

I jammed the key in the ignition and peeled out of the company's parking lot. For the rest of the day, I helped Vince with a domestic case that turned fatal. Stan and I barely spoke.

# SIXTEEN

That night, Hank called. I'd forgotten what a deep voice he had. And there went that flutter in my stomach again.

"Loved meeting you the other night," he said. "I don't have Jack with me this weekend, and Firehouse 12 is having one of their Sanctuary Sunday concerts—contemporary jazz. All the proceeds are going to the 'Kids Read' program. I was wondering if you'd like to go with me. The food's decent, and the jazz is usually great."

I grinned. "Now, how did you know I'm a jazz fan?"

"Well, I might have interviewed Melissa."

"Why am I not surprised? Yes, I'd love to go. And thanks for the invite."

"How about if I pick you up around seven? Does that work?"

"Perfect." I gave him my address, and we chatted for a few more minutes. He was so easy to talk to.

Admit it, I told myself. You like him. How could that be? I was in love with Chet, obsessed with the guy, wasn't I? Huh… something to talk to my therapist about at our appointment tomorrow.

———

The next morning, Stan didn't show up for work and hadn't called in. What the hell? I tried his cell three times and was sent to voicemail. This was not good. This was so not good. My pulse ratcheted up several notches, as my messages got increasingly desperate. "Please, Stan, I'm worried. Call me immediately and let me know you're okay."

I waited another ten minutes. Nothing. I picked up my purse and jogged out to my car and headed to his place.

When I pulled up at the small starter home in Hamden that he and his ex-wife had bought together, I saw his car in the driveway. I banged on the door. Over and over. No answer. I looked in all the usual places for a spare key—under the mat, the planter on the porch that held a wilted and very dead plant, and on top of the molding above the door. My heart pounded. No time to wait for a locksmith. I ran back to my car, grabbed my nightstick, raced back to the door, and smashed it open.

The place was a holy mess. It stank of beer and rotted food. Crumpled cans and fast-food wrappers littered the living room.

"Stan," I screamed. "Where are you?"

No answer. And then I saw him. He was lying on the kitchen floor, a pool of vomit by his head. *Oh my God, oh my God, oh my God!*

I rushed over and bent down, nearly overcome by the stench. He was barely breathing. His skin had taken on a deathly pale, bluish tinge. He felt cold, clammy. I rolled him onto his side and pulled his arms overhead as I'd been taught in training so he wouldn't choke on his own vomit.

I yanked out my phone and called for help. "Please come quick. My partner's passed out, and his breathing is labored, uneven." I ran into his bedroom and yanked a blanket off his bed, and returned to the kitchen to drape it over him.

My whole body trembled as I waited for the EMTs. They arrived in less than seven minutes, minutes that felt interminable. They gave him oxygen, got an IV going, and loaded him into an ambulance. I followed them in my car to the emergency room at Yale New Haven Hospital. I parked and dashed inside, only to be told the doctors were working on him, and I needed to stay in the waiting room.

I sat down on an orange plastic chair in the corner and rocked back and forth. Funny. I'd left the Catholic Church years ago, but now I found myself praying hard. *Please don't let him die, God. Please.* In between prayers, I beat myself up for not having told Captain Singleton what was going on with Stan. He liked the guy. He would have gotten him into treatment right away. Now my partner's life might be over, or he might have permanent damage, and it would be my fault.

Forty-five minutes later, a gray-haired physician with lines of fatigue etched on his face emerged into the waiting room. "Lieutenant O'Connor," he called out.

I rushed over. "I'm O'Connor," I said.

He extended his hand. "I'm Doctor Gathani. Your partner's a lucky man that you found him when you did. He could easily have choked on his own vomit with this level of alcohol poisoning."

"But he's going to be all right?"

"I expect him to fully recover. We've pumped his stomach. We're giving him vitamins and glucose to raise his blood sugar and prevent seizures. Fortunately, any permanent damage is unlikely. We'll keep him overnight, and then he should be good to go."

I wanted to throw my arms around him, but I controlled myself. "That's such a relief, Doctor. I can't tell you how grateful I am."

"Yes, well, this appears to be the result of binge drinking, which, as you know, is extremely dangerous. Have you noticed him drinking more than usual?"

"I have. We've talked about it, but he's resisted getting help. And I've been kicking myself for not reporting his drinking to our boss. I'm going to call him now."

"Good. Once he recovers from this, your partner needs treatment. The sooner the better."

"Agreed. When can I see him?"

"We're moving him to a room in the next few minutes. Once we get him settled, you can visit him."

"Sounds good. Will the front desk know his room number?"

He assured me they would.

I retreated to a corner of the hallway outside the waiting room to call Captain Singleton. I dreaded telling him what was going on, but worse would be not letting him know. I'd been doing that for far too long.

He picked up right away and growled, "Where the hell are you, O'Connor? And where's Stan?"

My voice shook as I told him we were at the hospital. "Stan has severe alcohol poisoning, sir, but the doctor expects him to make a full recovery, thank God."

"What the fuck? Was he binge drinking?"

"Yes, apparently. I couldn't reach him this morning, so I went over to his house and found him unconscious."

"Has he been making a habit of drinking too much?"

I swallowed hard. "He has."

"For God's sake, O'Connor. Why didn't you tell me? Has this been going on since his wife left?"

"Pretty much. It's gotten a lot worse lately. We've talked about it, and I've been encouraging him to go to AA, get help, but he hasn't wanted to."

"Well, he's got no choice now. He's going into treatment whether he likes it or not. And he's suspended. And I want to see you in my office this afternoon. I'm not happy with how you handled this, O'Connor."

"I understand, sir. I'm so sorry."

"You should be." He clicked off.

So much for my sterling reputation as the star of the homicide department. I'd managed to demote myself to jerk of the precinct.

I had the presence of mind to call and leave a voicemail canceling my appointment with Dr. Stein and headed over to the front desk, where a blue-haired lady with heavily powdered cheeks and a warm smile directed me to where they'd moved Stan—fifth floor, 524.

When I got to his hospital room, the only sounds came from the machine monitoring his heart rate and blood pressure. Stan's eyes were half-closed.

"Hey partner, Dr. Gathani says you're going to make a full recovery."

"Wha... what happened?"

"You passed out from alcohol poisoning. When I couldn't reach you this morning, I went over to your house and found you."

His face twisted in pain. Or maybe distress. "Great," he mumbled. "Just great."

"Can I get you anything?"

He shook his head.

"Anyone you want me to call?"

"Nope. This is humiliating enough without broadcasting my problems to the world."

Personally, I didn't think calling his parents or Joey Luongo, his close friend from his old Brooklyn neighborhood, amounted to "the world." But I understood he felt embarrassed about his life unraveling, even if this amounted to a temporary blip and not a permanent condition.

I decided to try to sound reassuring. "Doc says I can spring you out of here in the morning."

"Okay. Does Captain Singleton know?"

"Yeah." I bit my lip. "I had to call him, Stan. He's very concerned."

He pulled his hand away from mine. "Why didn't you just tell him I took a sick day? Geez, Caitlin, you didn't have to rat me out."

"I had to tell him. Stan, you could have killed yourself! Like it or not, Captain has ordered you into treatment."

"Terrific. You've single-handedly ruined my reputation in the department. Captain will probably fire me now or I'll be back on parking-ticket patrol, thanks to you."

Heat flooded my neck and face. "He wants to arrange treatment, not can or demote you. Look, I get I'm on your shit list. Well, take your place in line! Captain is angry at me for not reporting your drinking problem."

"And if I don't want treatment?"

"Not an option."

# SEVENTEEN

When I tapped on Captain Singleton's door frame that afternoon, he growled at me to shut the door and take a seat.

I sat.

"I've spoken to HR. They're going to set Stan up with a short-term treatment program. If that doesn't work, he'll go to 90-day residential if he wants to keep his badge."

"I know he does. That sounds... good." God, I sounded lame.

"What I'd like to know, Lieutenant, is whether I've ever done or said anything to you that would make you think you couldn't come to me with something this serious?"

"No, sir. It's my fault."

"Why didn't you report this to me before your partner nearly died?"

I bit back tears. "I... I guess I felt like I'd be a snitch to my partner. And he kept insisting he didn't want or need help."

He cracked his knuckles. "But you knew he was in trouble, didn't you? And a cop with a drinking problem is a danger, not only to you as his partner, but to the public he's sworn an oath to protect and serve. In this case, you used extremely poor judgement. Frankly, I'm very disappointed in you."

My stomach sank to somewhere around my knees. "I truly am sorry, sir. I take full responsibility."

He sighed. "All right then. I'm putting a note about this in your file. I'm giving you a break here because of your excellent record for the past twelve years. But I'm warning you, Caitlin. Do not keep anything like this from me again, or the consequences will be much more serious. Are we clear?"

I gulped and managed to get out a "Yes, sir."

He nodded. "Let's leave it then. Update me on the Miseau case. Are we any closer to finding out what killed her?"

I filled him in on the possibility that she'd come in contact with something that could have stopped her heart but wouldn't have shown up in the toxicology tests. "We're testing her costumes and warm up clothes right now—still waiting on the results."

"All right. Keep me posted."

That afternoon, I felt lower than low. And I was mad at everybody. First on the list was Stan for nearly killing himself. I knew about alcoholism—it was a disease, and resistance to getting help was part of the illness. But I was pissed at him anyway, even if I had no right to be. And I was angry at Captain Singleton for dressing me down and confirming my worst fears about myself. I really was a loser. Mostly, I was disgusted with myself. Captain was right. My judgment stank to high heaven.

I put in a call to Dr. Stein and got voicemail again. I apologized for the last-minute cancellation and asked if we could reschedule. She called back half an hour later and suggested I come at six that night for a make-up appointment.

I thanked her and said I'd be there.

———

When I arrived at Dr. Stein's, I breathed in the lavender scent of her candle and took in her gorgeous plants, her flowered spring dress, and her warm smile—all amounting to one startling contrast to my mood. I plopped down on her couch and heaved a heavy sigh. "Thanks again for seeing me."

"I gathered you were having a hard day." As she gazed at me intently, she knit her fingers together and folded them beneath her chin.

"My grandmother used to say, 'Nothing happened but the dog died.' That about sums up my day, my week—hell, my month."

"Let's start with today."

I went through the horror of discovering Stan unconscious from alcohol poisoning, the terror of thinking he might die, followed by relief that he'd recover. "Of course, now he's furious at me for telling our boss about his drinking problem and getting hospitalized. Captain Singleton's ordering him into treatment."

Just going through it all again brought tears to my eyes. "And then," I told her in a shaky voice, "my boss raked me over the coals for not immediately reporting my concerns about Stan's drinking. Told me flat out he was disappointed in me and my poor judgment."

"How do you feel about your judgment?"

"He's right. I'm such a jerk."

"We all make decisions we wish we could take back, Caitlin. Help me understand why you chose to keep this information from your boss."

I took a deep breath. "First off, I didn't want to feel like a snitch. And Stan said if I reported him, he'd tell the captain I was having an affair with the very married medical examiner."

"So basically, he extorted your silence."

"You could say that, I guess. To be really honest, I've been somewhat of a golden girl in the department because of my track record for closing cases. I didn't think I would necessarily lose my job if my boss found out about my involvement with Chet. But he definitely wouldn't have approved."

"And I gather his approval means a lot to you."

"Yeah. And as it turned out, I lost his approval anyway because of not telling him about Stan. Not to mention I nearly let my partner die."

"What I'm noticing is how hard you are on yourself. You were not the one who chose to drink in excess. That's on Stan."

"He has a disease. What's my excuse?"

"You do know the old saying about hindsight, don't you? That it's twenty-twenty? You chose not to divulge your partner's excessive drinking, which in retrospect, you feel was the wrong decision. But obviously on the job, you've made lots of great decisions in your investigations which have resulted in positive outcomes. One bad decision does not a jerk make." She smiled at me, seemingly pleased with her own play on the word I'd used to describe myself.

I tried to smile back, but I still felt lousy about myself.

"You know, Caitlin, we all like approval and acceptance from others. But my sense is your boss's opinion of you feels especially crucial and colors how you feel about yourself. What do you think?"

I shrugged. "I guess. Obviously, I don't feel great about how I've handled my personal life. My work has been the one area where I've felt good about myself. Today was... well, devastating. And it hasn't helped that the case I'm working on seems to be going nowhere fast."

"One more reason for you to be down on yourself, I gather."

"For sure. And I've now gotten two threatening phone

calls from some creep disguising his or her voice in the middle of the night telling me they want me to die."

"Good heavens. That's awful. Have you reported them?"

"Yeah. I filed a report. I haven't really talked to Captain Singleton about them, because... well... he might ask me who has a grudge against me personally, and my guess would be Chet's wife, Marian."

"You think she's responsible?"

"I have no idea. Part of me thinks there's no way because she'd have to have purchased special equipment she's hidden from her family, she'd have to stay up, et cetera. But part of me wonders. Both calls happened shortly after I'd spent time with Chet."

"Interesting. Well, I hope they stop. And what's going on with Chet?"

"I dropped in on him to ask about an investigation and ran into him and his wife returning from lunch. They were chatting and laughing. After she left, he tried to tell me he was just pretending to be happy with her, that I was all that he thought about, yada, yada."

"How did that make you feel?"

"Like a stupid jerk."

She smiled. "There's that word again."

Even I smiled this time. "Yeah, my word of the week."

"You think you might be ready to take a break from him and from being so hard on yourself?"

"That's just it. I always think I'm ready. It's the follow-through that gives me trouble."

"We'll look at that. Anything else of note happen since our last session?"

A picture of Hank floated across my mind. "As a matter of fact, I met someone interesting Saturday night. I had dinner with Melissa, my closest friend, and her husband. They brought along a guy named Hank, another teacher from the middle school where Melissa teaches. He's divorced, shares custody of his son, a really nice guy. He's invited me to go to a jazz concert on Sunday night."

She leaned forward. "Wow. Sounds nice. Do you feel attracted to him?"

"Actually, yes. I felt a little confused because I know I'm still hung up on Chet, and yet, I was drawn to Hank."

Dr. Stein's eyebrows lifted. "It's certainly possible to be attracted to more than one person," she said. "It's what we do with these attractions that matters. And sometimes being attracted to someone outside of your current attachment is a symptom of a problem in that relationship."

I held my hands up. "We have a problem all right. Chet's not really available. He's married to Marian, and they looked perfectly happy when I saw them together."

"Did you do any more thinking about the payoff you get from being involved with him since he's a married man?"

"Still working on it. Maybe it feels safer to me because it doesn't interfere with my career. I get to feel needed and wanted while my life continues on my terms."

She nodded. "It sounds to me, though, that it doesn't always feel great."

She had me there. I sagged into the couch cushion. "True."

"Suppose this new relationship with Hank develops. How would you feel about being with someone who was fully available?"

"Excited.... Also scared shitless."

"That's honest. Next time, I'd like us to take a look at your experiences growing up. We may get some clues about where some of this fear is coming from."

I frowned. "I had amazing parents growing up," I said, feeling suddenly defensive.

"Great. So, we can talk about all the ways they were amazing, and more about why it is that you don't cut yourself much slack."

I wasn't sure why, but a ball of anxiety clunked against the walls of my stomach at the prospect of dissecting my childhood. Was it possible it wasn't as perfect as I'd always thought it was?

# EIGHTEEN

When I left Dr. Stein's office, I checked my messages. Chet had left a voicemail: "Working late tonight at the office. Can I come by?"

My throat felt uncomfortably dry as I pondered my response. Was I or wasn't I serious about taking a break from Chet? I drove back to my apartment slowly through patches of rain, thinking about my session with Dr. Stein. Time to get serious about changing my patterns.

When I got home, I poured myself a glass of wine, sank onto the couch, and messaged him. "No. This isn't helping either one of us."

"Can we talk about this?" he texted.

"No." If I could have turned off my cell, I would have. But as a cop, I didn't have that option. I settled for moving the phone into the hallway where I wouldn't be tempted to look at my messages. Then I fixed myself some toast and scrambled eggs and tuned in to an old *Seinfeld* episode.

Jerry and George were pitching a television series which, they explained, would be a totally fresh concept—it would be "about nothing." After all these years, the show still made me laugh. And oh, how I needed some humor in my life right now.

———

The next morning, I broke down and looked at my messages. Six more from Chet, pleading with me to let him come over, so we could talk. "Talking" with Chet never lasted long before we ended up in bed. At least for once, I'd stuck to my guns.

I did email him, however, when I got to work to ask if there was any news about the tests on Miseau's clothing.

"Nothing yet," he tersely replied.

Okay, so he was pissed I wasn't at his beck and call. Well, tough shit. I was standing up for myself. About time.

But I sure felt like I was in a holding pattern with this damned case. And I was worried about Stan. I checked with Captain Singleton about where I could reach him. He gave me the name and number of the short-term facility he'd checked him into but told me I couldn't talk to him for the first 48 hours minimum while he was detoxing.

I felt oddly bereft I couldn't talk to my partner. Even though we were not on the best of terms at the moment, I missed him—missed talking about our cases, bouncing ideas off one another, and even sharing fries at Wendy's.

For the rest of the week, while I waited for the toxicology results, I partnered up with Vince, working other cases. They were basically routine—but heartbreaking as well. A drunk driver had lost control of his vehicle and veered onto the sidewalk, killing a four-year-old boy on his tricycle, and severely injuring his mom.

Then there was the angry ex-husband who'd defied the protective order his former wife had taken out on him. He broke into her house where he shot and killed both her and her new boyfriend while they were getting ready for bed. Oh, and he also killed her dog. Nice guy. In this job, there were crimes that left me feeling sick to my stomach.

———

Friday afternoon, I got a surprise phone call from Mrs. Bisso, Stan's mother. "I just found out from Captain Singleton where my son is," she said. "I couldn't reach him, and I've been so worried. I'm relieved your captain has arranged for him to get treatment. Captain Singleton said if you hadn't gone over to check on him, he could have died. You may have saved his life, and I can't thank you enough."

My jaw dropped somewhere down around my chest. Captain Singleton had told her my actions might have saved Stan's life? He certainly had been singing a different tune when he reprimanded me in the office.

At least he'd taken up for me with Stan's mom, and for that, I was incredibly grateful. "Oh Mrs. Bisso, thank you for saying that. I've been so concerned about him. He took the end of his marriage hard, as you well know. I'm really hopeful that he'll embrace recovery fully."

"Me as well. I'm going to Mass every morning and praying for him."

"He's lucky to have you for a mom. He makes my mouth water every time he talks about your risotto."

"Ahh… he's a good boy. When he gets out, I want you to come to Brooklyn with him to dinner. I promise to serve risotto."

"Sounds great, but to be honest, I'm not his favorite person right now. He didn't want me to tell Captain about his drinking."

"Oh pshaw! That's the alcohol talking. He'll realize you did the right thing."

*If only I'd done it sooner.* "Thank you. I really appreciate your calling. I was going to try to call him tonight and see if I could visit him tomorrow."

"He can take calls, but he's not allowed visitors right now."

"I didn't realize that. I'll at least try to call."

———

Talking to Mrs. Bisso had made me so hungry for risotto that I picked some up from Giovanni's on the way home. It was good, but based on Stan's description, I was pretty sure it didn't measure up to his mom's version.

When I called him that night, he did not sound pleased to hear from me.

"You won't believe this God-awful place Captain stuck me in after you gave me up," he said. "Non-stop bullshit every day. Hours of group therapy with a bunch of losers, individual counseling sessions, lectures. It never stops."

"I know it's hard, Stan, but hopefully, it'll be worth it in the end."

"What end? As far as I'm concerned, life without booze is unbearable."

"Okay, but life with booze nearly killed you. Your mom called me today. She is so relieved you're getting help, and I am, too. People care about you, Stan. We're in your corner."

"You're not in the same corner with my mom, Caitlin. You're not even in the same ballpark. You're nothing like her, believe me. And when I get out of here, I'm seriously thinking about putting in a request for a new partner."

He'd done it—delivered a body blow that left me reeling, struggling to breathe. For several moments, I couldn't even form words. Finally, I got out, "That really hurts, Stan. I hope maybe by the time you get out, you won't feel that way."

"I doubt it," he said. And then he hung up.

I lost it. I sobbed uncontrollably.

When the phone rang. I clutched it, planning to let the call go to voicemail. But it was Melissa.

"Hey," I said, trying to sound like I hadn't just been bawling my eyes out.

"What's wrong?" She knew me way too well.

"It's my partner Stan." I went through what had gone down on Tuesday. "Now our boss has put him in treatment, and he hates it and blames me for reporting him. I just talked to him, and he says he's probably going to request a new partner. I feel so rotten. It hurts."

"I'm sorry, Cait. I just want you to try to remember whatever he says right now has much more to do with his issues than with anything about you. Hopefully, he'll change his tune once he gets further along in recovery. And if not, that's his loss. You've been a great partner to him."

I sighed. "I should have reported him sooner. The guy almost died. I feel guilty as hell."

"You remember how my mom used to quote Erma Bombeck?"

"I know, I know. 'Guilt is the gift that keeps on giving.' Trust me, my guilt has been on a regular spree."

Melissa snorted. "At least you haven't lost your sense of humor. Now let's talk about tomorrow night. I hear you've got a date with Hank."

"True. He's a nice guy."

"He's the best. So, what are you wearing?"

I laughed. "This is what you're worried about? What I'm wearing? I have no idea."

"Wear your periwinkle tunic. Looks fabulous on you."

"Thank you, Mother."

"Ha ha. Listen, one more thing."

"What?"

"Hank's one of my favorite people in the world. Please don't string him along if you're not really interested. He's been hurt enough."

"You know that's not my style. I'm going to be honest with him."

"Okay, but don't be too honest, Cait. You never know. You may change your mind about your obsession with Chet."

"Working on that, as a matter of fact... What did you mean about Hank having been 'hurt enough'?"

"His ex was never happy with him being a schoolteacher. She pressured him to go back to school, get into administration. But he wanted to stay in the classroom. And then she got involved with the vice-president of the insurance company where she worked and left Hank high and dry."

"Sounds a lot like what happened to Stan with his ex."

"It's going around. That's one of the reasons I thought you and Hank might get along. You're both dedicated to your work more than you are to money."

I looked around my apartment and all my Goodwill and garage sale finds—my 50s style red plaid armchair, Danish contemporary coffee table, and side table painted with flowers. "And I have my mix 'n match secondhand furniture to prove my dedication."

"Oh, come on, I love your place. It's... well, it's eclectic."

I smiled. "You do know how to cheer me up, my friend. I'm so glad you called. I love you, you know."

"As well you should. Have fun tomorrow night, okay?"

"That's the plan."

# NINETEEN

Before my big date with Hank, I had a Saturday lunch date with my mom. We were both busy, but we tried to get together every couple of weeks.

We met at Donovan's, my favorite café downtown. On the lower level of one of the city's oldest office buildings, the restaurant featured peach-painted stucco walls, a stone floor, and year-round strings of holiday lights hung across its low ceiling. It reminded me of a cozy cave.

"There you are," Mom said when I rushed in, ten minutes late.

"I'm so sorry. I lost track of time."

"It's no big deal. Remember how many times your dad would call up and say, 'Honey, not going to make it for dinner. Leave me something to warm up, okay?'"

"I remember. When Dad didn't come home, you always let us eat dinner in the living room while we watched *Jeopardy*. I still love that show."

The waiter came by and took our order—iced tea and spinach quiche for Mom and coffee and a turkey club for me.

After he left, I told Mom how great she looked. Which she did. In the year since Dad died, she'd joined a health club, cut her hair into a fashionable style, and invested in a new, much more colorful wardrobe. Today she wore a multi-colored print top and purple pants.

"Thank you, honey. I miss your dad terribly, but I've tried really hard not to be one of those pathetic widows who sits around all day feeling sorry for myself."

"I can't imagine you ever doing that. I can still see that calendar up on our kitchen wall with all your volunteer commitments while we were growing up. Was there anything you didn't do?"

The waitress set our drinks down and told us our food would be right out.

Mom took a sip of her iced tea. "Well, I never had the career I'd planned on. I know I told you I fell in love with sociology in college. I really wanted to go on to grad school and become a professor. But that wasn't what life had in store for me. Your dad came into the picture my senior year. We got married, and pretty soon, your brothers came along, and then you."

She sounded...well, wistful. My mom had seemed like such a force of nature when I was growing up. I never really thought about what she might have wanted to do instead of being a fulltime homemaker and community volunteer. "Did you ever think about going back to school after you'd had us?" I asked her.

"I did, but your father didn't think it was a good idea, given his long and unpredictable hours. And he was probably right."

"I always thought you chose not to work. I didn't realize Dad didn't want you to."

She shrugged. "You have to understand, your father grew up without a mother. He endured a lot of lonely years with a gruff dad who wasn't home much. One of the things he felt most strongly about was that his children should have a mom who was around."

"Do you wish now you hadn't had us, made different choices?"

She put her hand over mine. "Of course not! I wouldn't trade my children for the world. And I loved your father."

"I'm glad we're talking about this, because my therapist suggested I look at my childhood for clues about why I always seem to fall for unavailable men."

The waitress set our food down. Mom's quiche was steaming and smelled so good I wondered if I'd made the wrong choice. But the minute I bit into one of the café's home-made warm chips, I didn't regret ordering a sandwich.

"So, I gather you're still seeing Chet?"

"Working on taking a break from him and trying to figure out why I keep doing this to myself."

Mom took another bite of her quiche and looked thoughtful as she chewed. After swallowing, she said, "You were a daddy's girl. Think about it. Unlike your brothers who wanted nothing to do with joining the force, from the time you were little, you were determined to be a detective like your father. You used to say, 'I want to catch the bad guys like Daddy does.'"

I smiled at the memory. "But what does that have to do with falling for the wrong guys?"

"Well," she paused, "getting involved with unavailable men means you don't have to worry about being with anyone who wants more from you than an occasional evening. When you have a demanding career like yours, adding marriage and kids is not impossible, but it's definitely challenging. And your dad made it pretty clear that in his opinion, good mothers stayed home with their kids."

I sipped my coffee. "That's true, but he came from a different generation. I know plenty of women my age who are doing careers and families—look at Melissa."

"Absolutely, but sometimes we think one thing, and our emotions tell us another. And looking back, I think your dad sent you a lot of mixed messages. Remember the argument your father and I had about 'Take Your Daughter to Work Day' the year you turned twelve?"

I hadn't thought about that night in years. My brothers were at football practice, and Mom, Dad, and I sat around the family dinner table eating slices of Mom's famous homemade pizza when she brought up the upcoming 'Take Your Daughter to Work Day.' When Mom told my dad she wanted to take me to the Library Board meeting, he suggested I come to work with him instead. He wanted me to meet Kass Phillips, the new "whip smart" assistant district attorney.

I remember Mom's whole face closing up when he went on to talk about all the guys crushing on her in the office, but how she was "way too smart to get married and take her eyes off her career."

Boy, did that frost Mom who accused him of looking down on her because she'd foregone a career in favor of getting married.

He denied it, of course, but he sure was eager for me to meet Kass Phillips.

I pulled myself back to the present. "I remember, Mom. You're right. Dad did have some weird ideas about women. But I knew what you did mattered. You were always there for us. I had an amazing childhood."

Her eyes twinkled. "Yes, but of your two parents, guess who you really wanted to be when you grew up?"


That afternoon, I couldn't stop thinking about my mother's comments about my dad. I'd idolized him growing up and patterned my career after his. Why had I ignored the ways in which he'd discounted my mother? She was a fantastic mom and had done so much for her community for decades.

And yet, as I thought about it more, Dad had thrust her into a lose-lose situation. He didn't want her to have a career outside the home, but when push came to shove, he clearly expressed greater respect and admiration for highly successful career-oriented women. I knew he loved my mom. He told her all the time how beautiful she was and how lucky he was that she was the mother of his kids.

Still, he'd definitely sang the praises of professional women repeatedly. Even though he'd been gone for more than a year and I was in my late thirties, was *his* voice the one that I'd internalized? On some level, did I think I couldn't really be worthy unless I devoted myself to my career and skipped marriage and motherhood?

I'd always dismissed introspection and self-reflection as "a lot of belly-button gazing," but I was starting to realize doing the work I'd begun with Dr. Stein in therapy was long overdue.

Right now, though, I had something to get ready for—my first date with Hank. I pulled out my periwinkle tunic and a long black skirt and boots before jumping in the shower.

———

Hank showed up right on time, looking handsome in his sky-blue turtleneck and jeans. I inhaled a whiff of his aftershave, which smelled delicious. "Armani?" I guessed.

"*Acqua di Gio*," he said. "My mom gave it to me for Christmas. What do you think?"

"I think your mom has excellent taste."

"And so do you. I love your top."

"Melissa gave me strict instructions about what to wear."

"Great choice." He looked around my apartment and smiled appreciatively. "I take it you're not wed to any particular decorating style. I love it."

"You don't get this particular look without a lot of trips to Goodwill and consignment shops."

"Huh… I'll have to try that. It's very cozy… and unpre-dictable."

"That's one word for it," I said with a laugh.

————

Firehouse 24 was one of my all-time favorite places. The only club in the state devoted exclusively to live jazz, its acoustics were amazing, as was its ambiance. The refurbished firehouse featured sloped high beam ceilings, brick walls, and floor to ceiling windows. We settled on a comfy couch and ordered a bottle of cabernet and a couple of Italian *piadina* flatbread sandwiches. We talked about music and what groups we liked before Bill Frisell's *Beautiful Dreamers* came on to do a set. They played original music, and the combination of their lead guitarist, the violist, and a drummer was unusual. Truthfully, I was a fan of old school Dixieland jazz and torch songs from the American Songbook, but these guys had such a fresh sound, and I loved how they played off each other.

"How did you get so interested in jazz?" Hank asked during the break between sets.

"My great-uncle played jazz trumpet in a local combo, and my dad used to take the whole family to his performances. And then in college, some friends and I went to the Newport Jazz Festival. After that, I was totally hooked."

"I've always wanted to go to that." He leaned forward and touched my arm. "Maybe we can go together this summer." His intense gaze locked on to mine.

My heart skittered. He was clearly declaring his interest in me, but what did I have to offer him? He was such a nice guy. The last thing I wanted to do was lead him on.

I cleared my throat. "Hank, to be honest with you, there's someone else in my life. I don't think it's a permanent thing, but it means I'm not really in the market right now for another relationship."

He pulled back and lifted his wine glass to take a sip. His gaze lingered on mine, a solemn look on his face. "Okay, I understand. But I like you. And since you did say this other person is probably not a permanent fixture in your life, I don't see any reason why we can't enjoy spending time together, becoming friends. If that's okay with you, that is."

Relieved that I'd been upfront with him, and he wasn't running away, I grinned at him and said, "That's very okay with me."

———

As I got ready for bed that night, I thought about the evening with Hank. He was so easy to talk to and be with.

Of course, maybe he wasn't that interested in me. He hadn't even tried to kiss me good night when he'd walked me to my door. I wondered what it meant that I felt a little disappointed—even though I'd told him I wasn't in the market for anything more than friendship.

———

I dreamed someone was banging on my door, and it took me a couple of minutes to realize it wasn't a dream. I looked at the clock. 2:00 a.m.. What the hell?

I groggily moved to the door. It had to be Chet. Who else would dare to pay a call on me in the middle of the night? I peered through the peephole.

"Caitlin, please. Let me in," he yelled.

I opened the door. "Shhh. You'll wake the neighbors."

He stumbled in and pulled me into his arms. "Thank God you're here," he said, tightening his grip around me. "I dropped by earlier tonight. Where were you?"

A flash of irritation coursed through me. What right did this guy with a wife and two kids have to know how I spent my time? "I was out," I said, flatly. "A friend and I went to listen to some jazz at Firehouse 24."

"A male friend?"

"Chet, what business is this of yours? In case you've forgotten, you're married to someone else."

"I know, I know. But what we have is so different. It's more than how beautiful it is to make love to you."

"What do you mean?"

"It's being with you, talking to you about work—your work, my work. My wife doesn't even want to hear about my cases. She says it's too 'disturbing.' I can't stand being with someone whose only idea of stimulating conversation is what color we should paint the dining room. Please, Cait. I need you. I don't want to let you go."

"You also don't want to let your wife and kids go. You've made that clear, and I haven't asked you to. But maybe I'm ready for something more in my life, something healthier, fuller."

He sprinkled a line of kisses on my neck then and whispered, "Tell me you don't want me, and I'll leave."

"Not the point," I said, just before he crushed his mouth on mine. He kissed me over and over, and pretty soon, I forgot all about what the point had been. My body did what it always did—responded to him, wanted him to touch me, wanted to touch him. Everywhere.

# TWENTY

The sun streaming through the slats of my blinds woke me the next morning. My middle-of-the-night lover was gone, and I felt like a world class whore. What was wrong with me? Why did I keep falling into bed with someone married to someone else, someone who would never really be there for me?

And that crap about how much it meant to him that we could talk about our work? Sure, we did have amazing conversations about cases. But what came first whenever we were alone? It was never analyzing our investigations.

I heaved myself up and plodded over to the coffeemaker. Chet had left a note on the counter: "Had to go. Last night was amazing. YOU are amazing." He'd drawn a heart beneath the message.

Amazing, huh? So amazing I was the original disposable lover, available to be fucked on demand before he went home to his adorable wife and kids?

I crumpled up his note and threw it in the trash. It was official. I could barely stand myself. Or him.

---

I dragged myself through the day, managing to get the laundry and grocery shopping done before the start of the work week. Hank called around five to say how much he'd enjoyed our get-together the night before.

Guilt prickled at me about my post-date tryst with Chet, even as I told Hank I'd had a good time, too. Which I had.

"I've got Jack with me this week and weekend through Sunday afternoon, but are you up for getting together next Sunday night for dinner?"

I didn't hesitate. "I'd love to."

"Any special requests?"

"Well, I never met an Italian dish I could resist."

"I have just the place."

We talked for a few more minutes, and I realized I was looking forward to seeing him again. Maybe there really was life after Chet.

———

My phone startled me awake at 3:00 a.m. that night. Once again, when I picked up, the first thing I heard was heavy breathing. And then that damned distorted voice: "Not getting the message, are you? I'll have to do something about that."

"Listen, you creep, I will figure out who you are, and there will be consequences," I shouted into the phone.

But all I heard in response was a click. The jerk had hung up.

This couldn't be a coincidence, could it? Another phone call the night after I'd been with Chet? Time to talk to him about his wife. Maybe he wasn't the only one in the marriage with a busy nocturnal life.

———

Monday morning, despite my interrupted sleep, I forced myself to do my three-mile run. I'd been slacking off lately, and as much as I hated the thought of jogging beforehand, it did clear my head, and I felt better afterward.

Of course, feeling better turned out to be short-lived. I'd barely downed my first cup of coffee at my desk before Tony, our forensics specialist, called to tell me all the tests on Lydia Miseau's costumes had come back negative—no sign of anything on them that could have made her ill.

I swore under my breath. "I can't believe we still don't know what killed her. I'm beyond frustrated."

"Wish I had better news for you."

I called Chet to discuss the discouraging news we'd gotten from Tony. "Any other ideas for me?"

"Not offhand. I'm really sorry, Cait." He lowered his voice. "I had a wonderful time the other night."

I didn't respond.

"You there?"

"I've been meaning to talk to you about these threatening phone calls I've been getting, Chet."

"What phone calls? You didn't tell me about this!"

"The day after the last three times we've seen each other, someone has called me in the middle of the night, using one of those distorted voice things, and telling me I deserve to die, and maybe they'll have to do something about that."

"Oh my God, that's awful. Have you reported it? Can they trace the calls?"

"Of course, I've reported it, and no, no luck yet tracing the calls. They're from different burner phones bought with cash that my friendly caller throws out in various locations around the city. But the timing is awfully coincidental, don't you think?"

"What are you saying? That Marian's behind these calls? That's impossible. One, she doesn't know about us, and two, she would never do something like that."

"I wouldn't be so sure your wife doesn't know."

A long silence hung between us. Finally, he said, "Well, I am. And there's got to be an explanation that doesn't involve my wife."

I sighed. Talking to Chet had left me exactly nowhere, either professionally or personally. "Gotta go," I said, and clicked off.

I decided to do what I always did when a case stumped me —go back to the scene and take another look. The stage where Lydia Miseau had died had long since been cleared for company performances, but I'd kept her dressing room cordoned off.

Dora, her hair newly styled in multi-colored corn rows, greeted me when I arrived. "No sidekick today?" she asked.

"Not today." I wondered if Stan was still furious at me and intended to dump me as his partner. Nothing to do but wait it out.

"Company class is about to start, so if you want to see Victor, you'll have to wait."

"That's okay." I headed downstairs to the dressing rooms and ducked beneath the tape around Lydia Miseau's door. A pile of beat-up looking pointe shoes lay in the corner. Notes from well-wishers and fans were taped to the edges of her makeup mirror. I studied the array of cosmetics on the counter: false eyelashes, jars of makeup, cleansing cream, mascara, rouge, eyeliner, and lipsticks. My mind drifted back to Melissa's and my theater days in high school. How we'd labored to get our makeup just right.

That's when it hit me. I couldn't believe I hadn't thought of this before. Lydia Miseau had been in full makeup for the final dress. What if someone had done something to her makeup? My heart raced. This could be it. *Please God, please, let this be it.* I pulled out my gloves and several evidence bags from my suit pocket and stuffed them with Lydia's cosmetics.

———

On the way out of the dressing room, I ran into Gus, the custodian. His dark brown eyes were doing that darting around thing again, as though he were scared to make eye contact with me. I wondered if I made him nervous or whether he'd once had a bad experience with the cops.

"Find anything?" he asked, clearly looking at the evidence bags I was carrying.

"I sure hope so... Say, Gus, have you ever noticed anyone going into Ms. Miseau's dressing room when she wasn't in there?"

"Sure. Kathy came in sometimes to drop off costumes. Victor's ex was in and out of all the dressing rooms photographing for that project she was doing. And Victor sometimes went in. He liked surprising her with flowers. Before she arrived, on that last day, he left her a beautiful bouquet. Probably still in there—at least what's left of them."

*Interesting.* "Okay, thanks. You have a good day."

"You, too," he called.

I walked down the hall and just before I began my climb up the stairs, I turned around to wave at Gus. But he was gone.

In my car, I called forensics and spoke to Tony again. "Bringing in Lydia Miseau's makeup. Need you to test for anything that might have been added to it."

"You don't give up easily, Caitlin."

"True."

———

That afternoon, Captain Singleton called me into his office for a "talk." The scowl on his face the last time he'd summoned me was gone, but he looked somber. "Caitlin, I know how much you hate giving up on a case, but it's time to let the

Miseau investigation go. Vince is still green and needs your help. Cases are piling up, and there's no point in our investigating a suspicious death if we can't figure out how it happened."

"I have one last idea I really want to check out, Captain." I explained about the possibility that something could have been absorbed in Lydia's skin that couldn't be detected in our toxicology tests. "Nothing showed up on her costumes, but I just submitted her makeup to Tony. If this doesn't pan out, I promise to move on."

He rubbed his chin. Finally, he said, "All right, but while you're waiting for the results, I want you to work with Vince on his cases. He looks up to you, you know."

"Nice to hear." Truthfully, working with Vince always made me miss Stan even more. For one thing, fresh-faced Vince with his rash of freckles looked about twelve and made me feel ancient. For another thing, he never ventured an opinion until I'd offered mine.

"Have you heard anything from Stan?"

"Not directly, but his mother called me. Said he's doing much better. Might even get out at the end of this week."

"Wow. That was fast." My pulse raced. The way my life was going, once released from treatment, Stan's first official act would be to request a new partner.

"That's why they call it short term treatment, O'Connor."

"Right. Anything else, sir?"

"One last thing. When Stan gets out, if there are any signs of a relapse, I expect you to come to me immediately."

"Of course." What I didn't say was I wasn't sure Stan and I would still be partners.

———

That night, Melissa called to get the lowdown on my date with Hank.

"It was good. He's such a nice guy. And I was honest with him about there being someone else, and he still wants to spend time together."

"Oh, okay," she said, sounding deflated. "At least, you didn't turn him off completely."

"I didn't. We're going out to dinner Sunday night."

Her voice perked up. "Great. He's really a special guy, Cait. I wish you could see him in action at school with the kids. And he's an amazing father."

"I get it. You don't have to sell him to me. The timing is just difficult right now. I'm trying to figure this whole thing out with Chet."

"What's to figure out? The guy's cheating on his wife and is not about to leave his kids. There's no future in this for you."

"I hear you. But emotionally, I'm all over the place. I wish I were as together and grounded as you are, but I'm not. However, you'll be glad to know I'm seeing Dr. Stein again tomorrow."

"Good. Now tell me the truth. Did you feel any sparks with Hank?"

I hesitated. "Is this just between us?"

"Of course."

"I did… And that scares the hell out of me."

"You need to stop getting in your own way. You deserve a good guy like Hank. Sometimes I want to shake you and tell you to stop sabotaging your own shot at something really wonderful, someone really wonderful. Trust me on this. Hank is the real thing. Do you hear me?"

"I hear you. This is something I have to figure out on my own." *Like I was so great at that.*

# TWENTY-ONE

Gus's wife had fallen asleep on their living room couch watching a rerun of *Law and Order.* He went into the bedroom, closed the door, and sank down on the bed. Could he really do this? But what choice did he have? Mary was his world, his life. He couldn't bear to lose her.

At least he had an idea what to say from all those crime shows Mary loved. Plenty of bad guys to imitate. He took a deep breath and made the call. "I seen what you did," he said. "That lady detective was sniffing around Miss Miseau's dressing room today. I know she'd be very interested in what I saw."

"I don't know what it is you thought you saw, but let me assure you you're mistaken."

"I don't think so. My wife is ill, and I could use some help with the bills. The way I see it, you can do a good deed making a contribution."

"What are we talking about here?"

"I'm going to need a down payment of $5,000."

"And then?"

"Depends on how much her treatment ends up costing us.

I figure my keeping quiet about what I seen should be worth a lot to you."

"All right. But I don't know how much more I can give you after the $5,000."

"We'll see about that." Gus gave instructions on where to leave the cash for pickup, the back door of an abandoned warehouse in the west end of the city. "Tomorrow night at eight," he said. "Don't be late."

# TWENTY-TWO

Dr. Stein greeted me warmly as she ushered me into her office for my Tuesday therapy appointment. She was so tiny I towered over her before we sat down. But as usual, her demeanor was powerful. And I loved her colorful wardrobe. Today she wore a chartreuse and lavender abstract scarf that reminded me of a painting I'd seen the last time I'd visited Boston's Museum of Fine Arts.

"What's been happening?" she asked, as she lit a candle.

I inhaled the scent of lavender and told her about my last-ditch effort to stay on Miseau's case and my worries about Stan getting out of treatment and threatening to request a new partner.

"Would that be so terrible?" she asked.

"It would feel like getting dumped, and I've gone through too much of that. And one more professional failure—my own partner saying he can't stand working with me. Plus, when Stan's on his game, we work really well together. And we're friends—at least we were."

"It's very possible that he'll feel differently about trading you in, so to speak, if he genuinely embraces recovery."

"Maybe." I wondered if Dr. Stein was being a little too optimistic.

"Anything else going on you'd like to talk about?"

A surge of heat worked its way up from my neck to my face. "Not sure I want to talk about this, but I probably should."

"Go on."

I told her about my date with Hank and how I'd been honest with him that there was someone else in my life, but he still wanted to see me. "I came home, and I was feeling good about myself. And then... then Chet came over in the middle of the night, and we ended up in bed together. I feel like that character in *Oklahoma* who sings, 'I'm Just a Girl Who Can't Say No.'"

Dr. Stein laughed. "I didn't know anybody your age even knew that musical."

"We did it in high school."

"Okay. So, I take it you didn't feel great about sleeping with Chet again."

"I felt slutty and shitty the next morning. I still feel awful about it—like I have no backbone. I keep asking myself why I'm doing this—and coming up empty. Oh, and one more thing. I got another creepy phone call threatening me—third one I've gotten the night after I've been with Chet. He claims it couldn't possibly be his wife, but I'm not big on coincidences, especially the third time around."

Dr. Stein leaned forward. "That sounds very scary. And you're right about coincidences. If Chet's wife does know about you, does that change things?"

I twisted my hands in my lap. "I don't know. Maybe. If she is the one making these phone calls, she's got to be pretty desperate to hang on to her marriage. I don't want to hurt anybody."

"It sounds like one of the people getting hurt right now is

you. Have you done any more thinking about why you've ended up in affairs with married men?"

"Actually, I had a really interesting conversation with my mom. She reminded me of times when my dad went on and on about professional career women he admired, even though he demanded my mom stay home."

"Tell me more."

I described my memory of the argument my parents had about the "Take Your Daughter to Work Day."

"What did you make of that at the time?"

"I remember feeling bad for my mom. I hated it when they argued. But I really wanted to be one of those career women my dad admired. And I wanted to follow in his footsteps and be great at my job."

"It sounds like he sent a pretty strong 'either-or' message. As a woman, either you forsook marriage and kids and devoted yourself to your career, in which case you earned his respect and admiration—or you married and stayed home to raise your family. You do realize most women with families work outside the home today?"

I nodded. "Of course, I know that. My dearest friend in the world does it all very successfully. But I never thought I could. And even though it doesn't make any sense, and my dad died more than a year ago, I still want to please him. I still want him to be proud of me."

"That's a very human and understandable emotion. We want our parents to be proud of us, to love us and accept us. But at some point, I think we have to ask ourselves about the cost of seeking a parent's approval, even one who's no longer here."

I shrugged. "Professionally, I'm doing exactly what my dad wanted me to do. But he certainly wouldn't have approved of my relationship with Chet if he'd known about it."

"The question is, 'Do you approve of it?'"

I threw my hands up. "Obviously not, and yet, I keep going down that same rabbit hole."

"That's true. Why do you think that is?"

I folded my arms around myself. "If I knew, I wouldn't be here in therapy."

"Fair enough. But let me throw something out there and see what you think. What if being involved with someone who's not really available is a way to stay safe?"

"I'm not following. I'm sure not feeling safe right now getting these creepy phone calls and feeling like total shit after being with Chet."

"Yes. But what I'm wondering about is if being involved with Chet is a way to get some affection and comfort in your life, even temporarily, while you still get to be your father's golden girl career-wise."

My mouth dropped open. "I never thought about it like that," I admitted.

"And I could be totally wrong. But I do want you to consider it as a possibility. And this week, I'd love for you to do some thinking about your own needs. If you took away the voices of important people to you—your parents, your boss, your partner, Chet, your best friend—what is it *you* would like to do and have in your life?"

At the thought of what I wanted for my life, apart from what others wanted for me, my mind went totally blank. Not a good sign.

———

I spent the rest of the week digging into Vince's cases and trying not to obsess over my worries about possibly having to give up on the Miseau case, Stan getting out of treatment, and why I kept coming up empty to the question Dr. Stein had asked me to think about.

Fortunately, Vince's cases were a great distraction, especially the woman who'd offered $20,000 to an undercover cop to kill her husband, a prominent tax attorney. She served on several charity boards in the city, and the couple appeared to be "idyllically happy." So much for appearances. Then there were the more routine cases—drug busts gone bad and another vehicular homicide due to drunk driving.

Thursday night, Chet called to say he was working late and wondered if he could "drop by."

My jaw clenched. "You know what, Chet? I'm pretty much done with drop-ins, pop-ins, whatever you want to call them. We need to take a break, while I figure out my life, and you figure out your marriage."

"Is that what you really want, Cait? I love you, you know."

I took in a sharp breath. "This isn't feeling like love. I don't know what it is, but I need you to stop coming over, stop calling me, unless it's about an investigation."

"Please, I need you." This was getting old. He sounded like a whiny kid begging for one more cookie.

"Right now, I'm working on what I need, Chet. And it's not this. It's not you."

I ended the call and felt like jumping up and down and clicking my heels. Had I really said that? Stood up for what I needed? And could I stick to it?

# TWENTY-THREE

Saturday morning, I was cleaning my apartment when my phone rang. I glanced down at my caller ID—it was Stan. I braced myself for what could be awful news.

"Hey," I said, tentatively.

"Hey yourself. I've been sprung."

"How do you feel?"

"Still a little shaky, but a lot better. Listen, Cait, I want to apologize for the stuff I said. You saved my life, and this has been a real wakeup call for me."

"You sound different. And it's so good to hear your voice," I said, biting back tears.

"I'm sorry I threatened to tell Captain Singleton about Chet and told you I wanted a new partner. I was such an asshole."

"You were, but I knew it was the alcohol."

"So, are we still partners?"

"Of course. You don't know how much I've missed you."

"Same here. Catch me up on what's been going on."

I filled him in on the latest with the Miseau case and the lurid details of Vince's attempted murder case.

"You know that's going to be a 'made for television movie,' right?"

"Definitely. I've already warned Vince *People* magazine will descend on him any minute."

Stan said he had to get off the phone to go to an AA meeting, but wanted to know if I was up for going to dinner in Brooklyn that night. "Mom wants to make risotto for you."

"You know I'd never turn down your mother's risotto. And Stan?"

"What?"

"Welcome back."

———

After talking to Stan, the heavy weight pressing on my chest miraculously lifted. He sounded so much better, and he'd actually apologized. *God is good*, I thought.

And the evening at his parents' house was joyful. Stan's skin had lost its grayish pallor, and his eyes were clear. I loved watching him with his mom, who clearly adored him. And his close friend Joey Luongo was there, telling tales of the pranks they'd pulled in middle school, including setting off the fire alarm. "Can you believe we both became cops?" he asked.

"Not really," I said.

Mrs. Bisso's risotto was every bit as delicious as Stan had claimed. I wasn't crazy about the non-alcoholic wine she served, but the toasts more than made up for it. My personal favorite was my own. "To new beginnings," I said, as Stan and I clinked glasses.

———

Hank showed up at my door five minutes early Sunday night. He had one of those smiles that took over his entire face. And he'd clearly tried to brush back his thick mass of curly black hair, which drifted in various directions, anyway. I liked that about him. Perfect looking people made me nervous.

"Blue must be your color," I said, taking in his light blue button-down shirt and navy sports jacket.

"Blame my mom. She always told me I should wear blue whenever I wanted to make a good impression." There was that mega-watt smile again.

A wave of warmth swept through me. I couldn't help smiling back at him. "She knew what she was talking about. So where are we going?"

"*Tre Scalini's.*"

"My mouth is already watering."


Located in downtown New Haven, *Tre Scalini's*, one of my favorites for special occasions, featured an elegant and intimate atmosphere with its wall of windows overlooking Wooster Street. But the best part was definitely its food.

Over a bottle of wine, we shared an antipasti dish to start. Once again, we took turns interviewing one another. He wanted to know what made me want to become a detective, how I felt about my job, and even my opinions about issues like police reform.

I really appreciated that he seemed as interested in knowing about me as I was in learning more about him. Maybe we were both inclined toward going into interview mode because of what we did for a living. Teachers and detectives both ask lots of questions.

"Enough about me," I said, after I'd told him about growing up as the daughter of a police chief and knowing I wanted to "catch the bad guys" just like my dad. "I want to know why you became a teacher."

"I think it was spending so much time at the YMCA when I was growing up. My dad was the Activities Director, and I hung out there all the time. I fell in love with basketball and got interested in coaching. By the time I was in high school, I was volunteering as an assistant coach in the recreational league for younger kids. Meanwhile, in school, I loved science. So, when I got to City University, it seemed like a natural fit to major in education and minor in biology. I knew if I went into teaching, I could also coach basketball."

"Sounds like you found a perfect fit for your interests," I said.

"I really did. I have a lot of friends I grew up with who hate what they do for a living, and I feel blessed that I get up every day and look forward to going to work."

"Your students are lucky. Middle school is tough, and I had some teachers who were so burned out."

"I get that. Middle schoolers are challenging. But you know, they're not so different from the rest of us. They're going through a lot. They want to feel heard, respected—and they want someone to tell them to cut the crap when needed."

I sipped my wine. "I think the whole emphasis on community policing is also about building connections so folks can feel heard. And my job is a lot about figuring out who's feeding me crap in an investigation, and who's being honest."

"How can you tell?"

"Sometimes you can't. But a lot of it is intuition. And my gut instinct that something doesn't feel right."

"That comes in handy for teaching, too," he said, "especially when you start to pick up that a kid is having a rough time at home, or with friends. They act out in all kinds of ways, and so often, the behavior is a symptom of something eating at them."

A thought flickered across my consciousness. Maybe my relationship with Chet was a symptom of something eating at me. I pushed the thought away, as the waiter came over and ran through the specials. They sounded good, but I went with my favorite, the spaghetti carbonara, while Hank decided on the linguini with little neck clams.

"How was your week with your son?" I asked Hank after the waiter departed.

"Good. He's into Legos, and we built a huge space station together."

"Very cool. Do you have any pictures?"

Hank pulled out his phone and scrolled through his photos. "I love this one." He handed me his phone. Jack stood proudly next to his dad as they both pointed to the space station they'd built. He was so cute—with a sprinkling of freckles across his nose, his dad's thick dark curls, and a tooth-gapped wide smile.

"He's adorable."

"Thanks. He's really special. I'm a lucky guy."

"I can tell. Is it tough to have to share him and send him back and forth?"

He sighed and wrinkled his forehead. "Truthfully, it sucks. I'd much rather have him with me full time. But it beats the alternative of not being in his life at all, or only having every other weekend with him."

"So, you have him half the time?"

"I do—one week with me, and one week with Mom. Jack's handled it pretty well. And we talk every day I'm not with him. It helps that my ex and I both live in the same school district."

The waiter arrived with our dishes, and we both dug in.

"This is so good," I said. "How's yours?"

"Fabulous, as is the company." His eyes gleamed in the candlelight, as he leaned toward me.

A sliver of heat wove its way up my chest. "Thank you. And I'd love to meet your son sometime."

He paused, fork in hand. "Maybe down the road. I'm always afraid he'll get attached to people who might not stay in his life, and I guess I'm your typical protective parent. I don't want to put him through any unnecessary losses."

"Understandable. Everyone should have a dad like you."

Color flooded into his face. "I really try."

"I can tell."

———

After dinner, we drove down to the harbor and took a long walk. The night air was unusually warm. I loved breathing in the saltwater scent and seeing the majestic cargo ships in the moonlight. It felt natural to take Hank's arm and match my steps to his.

And when he brought me home, he said, "I'd really like to see you again."

"That'd be great." Before I could even ask if he wanted to come in for a nightcap, he said goodnight and strode down the hallway to the stairwell.

Once again, he'd made no effort to kiss me. Since I'd made it clear to him that there was someone else in my life, I told myself I had no right to feel let down. But I was.

And when I checked my phone for messages, there were none from Chet. And no middle-of-the-night visits from him. This time, he'd clearly taken me at my word that I wanted him to leave me alone.

I still felt confused. Was that what I really wanted? Or was being with Chet like smoking—a bad habit I was attached to? Kicking it would mean going through the messy pain of withdrawal.

———

On Monday, Stan showed up right on time. All morning, other officers came by to welcome him back. He beamed at all the support. Shortly before noon, Captain Singleton called him into the office and a few minutes later, asked me to join them.

"Bisso tells me he's doing much better, and he has my permission to take time off as needed for AA meetings. I really want this to go well. For both of you. If you relapse, Bisso, I'm counting on you to inform me. Recovery can be uneven. And, O'Connor, you need to let me know if there are problems as well. None of this 'I didn't want to snitch on my partner' business. We're a team here, and we have to look out for one another. Clear?"

"Yes, sir," we said in unison.

When we got back to our desks, there was a message from Tony. "Just got the results on the makeup tests. Found something."

# TWENTY-FOUR

S tan and I hustled the three flights up to Tony's office, my pulse speeding up from the exertion. The moment we arrived, Tony stood up, all five feet four inches of him. He lifted his eyebrows, possibly the bushiest I'd ever encountered, and handed us a report.

"Long story short," he said. "We found traces of nitroglycerin in Miseau's makeup, enough to slow a healthy heart like hers until it simply stopped. And nitroglycerin flushes through the system fast, which is why it didn't show up in the toxicology tests."

Stan and I looked at each other and raised our own considerably less impressive eyebrows. This was big. And we both knew exactly who had access to nitroglycerin.

"Thank you so much, Tony." I grabbed the report, and Stan and I practically skipped down the stairs. "Finally, a break! If Captain signs off, I think we can officially rule this a homicide and bring Pesetsky in for questioning."

"Let's go see him now," Stan said.

"I feel like I've been saved from the firing squad—at least the squad that was going to fire us from pursuing this case."

Thirty minutes later, with Captain's blessing, we headed over to Ballet Études. We found Victor in his office with Frederick peering at what looked like financial statements spread across his desk. "Ah, Detectives," he said. "Any news?"

"Actually, there is, sir. Your wife's death was a homicide. We found traces of nitroglycerin in her makeup. We'd appreciate your coming with us to the station for questioning."

Victor's face went pale. "I can assure you I had nothing to do with my wife's death."

Frederick broke in. "Everyone knows my father takes nitroglycerin. Anyone could have come into this office and lifted some of his pills."

I turned to him. "Did you? You were seen going into Lydia's dressing room that morning."

"Frederick, what are they talking about?" Victor asked. I thought I detected a glimmer of suspicion as he stared at his son.

"It's nothing, Dad. I wanted to talk to her about a fundraising idea I had. You remember I told you I wanted to try something new? I wanted to call it *'Lunches with Lydia.'*"

"I think you mentioned something," he said.

Stan and I held the door and gestured to Victor to go through.

"I suppose this is my cue to call my attorney," he said stiffly.

"Good idea," I told him.

"I'll call Margolis, Dad, and have him meet you there," Frederick said.

"Tell him to hurry. And see if Alexander can teach company class today. Let everyone know rehearsals today are cancelled."

Frederick moved toward his father. "It's going to be okay, Dad."

Victor's face had gone from pale to gray. "One can only hope."

———

When we got to the station, we ushered Pesetsky into one of our interrogation rooms. He looked around at the windowless room that reeked of stale coffee and sweat, and curled his nose.

"Can we get you anything?" I asked.

He shook his head.

I Mirandized him, and he announced he wasn't saying a word until his attorney arrived.

We didn't have to wait long. In less than ten minutes, Ben Margolis, a short thick man with two clumps of side hair framing the bald top of his head, burst into the room like a bullfighter eager for time in the ring.

"What the hell is this about?" he demanded. "Why have you detained my client?"

"Mr. Pesetsky is a person of interest in the homicide investigation of his wife," I said.

"Homicide! I thought you people had not established cause of death."

"We discovered traces of nitroglycerin in Ms. Miseau's makeup, the same medication your client is on. Nitroglycerin was present in sufficient quantity to have shut her healthy heart down within hours."

Margolis snorted. "That's all you've got? How many thousands of people in this city are on nitroglycerin?"

"True, but your client not only had the means to kill his wife in his possession, but plenty of motive and opportunity as well."

"I had nothing to do with my wife's death," Pesetsky said.

Margolis turned to him. "Let me handle this, Victor." He glared at me. "What are you talking about?"

"Mr. Pesetsky had plenty of reasons to want to harm his wife. She carried on an affair with the company's lighting designer and was six weeks pregnant with his child when she died."

Pesetsky pulled a linen handkerchief out of his pocket and wiped beads of perspiration from his forehead. "I told you, Lieutenant, we were working things out. I forgave her."

Margolis grabbed his arm. "Don't say another thing, Victor. I mean it!"

"There's also the matter of a ten-million-dollar insurance policy on Lydia's life," I continued. "The ballet company was having serious financial problems, and the payout would obviously be extremely helpful. In addition, a witness saw Mr. Pesetsky enter Lydia's dressing room before she arrived on the morning of her death."

"To deliver flowers," Victor Pesetsky said.

Margolis shot him a stern look and then turned his attention to me. "So, all you've got is a bunch of speculation and some flimsy circumstantial evidence. Can you produce any witness who saw my client tamper with Ms. Miseau's makeup?"

"We're working on it," I said, deciding this was only a half-lie, given how nervous Gus had seemed whenever I'd talked to him. The custodian might have seen more than he was telling, perhaps fearful of being fired by Pesetsky if he spoke up. Especially with his wife being so ill, I was sure Gus wanted to hang on to his job.

"I don't think so," Margolis said. "Unless you're arresting my client, we're leaving."

"Be my guest." I turned to Pesetsky. "One more thing. Since you insist you had nothing to do with your wife's death, do we have your permission to search your home and office?"

"What can you possibly be looking for?" Pesetsky asked.

"The answer is no," Margolis said. "Not without a search warrant." He stood up, and Pesetsky followed suit.

"We'll be in touch, Mr. Pesetsky. Please don't plan on leaving the area," I said.

He nodded curtly, and the two men stalked out. Margolis slammed the door behind them.

Stan and I stared at each other. "What do you think?" I asked him.

He chewed his bottom lip. "Hell, Cait, like you said, we've got means, motive, and opportunity. Cases have been built on a whole lot less."

"Agreed. Let's get started on those search warrants. I want to submit them ASAP."

"You thinking Judge Randolph?"

"Yup. He helped us out bigtime on the kidnapping case."

By six p.m., we had our search warrants, specifically to look for any sort of pill crusher that Pesetsky might have used to grind up his heart medication. Judge Randolph had bought our argument that sooner was better than later. Murder suspects were generally eager to get rid of incriminating evidence.

"You up for a late night?" I asked Stan.

"Sure."

"Okay, how about if you and I search his house and ask Captain to assign two officers to search his office?"

"That works."

On the way to Pesetksy's house, we stopped at Wendy's and picked up a spicy chicken for me and a burger with the works for Stan, plus a large fry and two jumbo coffees. It was going to be a long night.

"Like old times," Stan said. "This feels good, you know? You and me on the hunt."

I grinned at him. "And I still love that you're always willing to share your fries."

# TWENTY-FIVE

Victor Pesetsky lived in a sprawling Victorian on the outskirts of the city. He glowered at us when we arrived and showed him our search warrant. He held a miniature poodle in his arms who was feverishly barking. "It's okay, Felicia." He turned his gaze on us. "Strangers make her a bit nervous at first."

"Any place she can go while we search?"

He sniffed. "I'll take her to the backyard, and she can stay there while you're here. How long is this going to take?"

"Maybe a few hours," I said.

"All right. I'm going out then." He handed me a card. "Please call my cell when you're done."

I nodded and asked him to point us to his kitchen. We walked across gleaming hardwood floors through high-ceilinged rooms filled with antiques and dance-related art. The framed Degas print of his *Dancing Class* was familiar, but I'd never seen the bronze sculpture of a ballerina in arabesque with her head thrown back in ecstasy. I wondered if the model had been his late wife.

The large kitchen appeared to be well used. Copper pots and pans hung over the central kitchen island, and books on

French and Mediterranean cooking lined an entire shelf over the small built-in desk adjacent to rows of glass-framed cabinets.

Stan and I gloved up and pulled out the pictures we'd retrieved online about the various pill crushers available on the market. They ranged from a pill mill capable of crushing multiple tablets into a fine powder, to an old-fashioned stainless steel and mortar pestle that also doubled as a spice grinder or useful implement for making pesto or guacamole. We'd also learned that some folks placed pills inside a plastic bag and bludgeoned them with a hammer, a method that was not recommended due to leakage problems.

I took one side of the kitchen, and Stan took the other. As far as I could tell, Miseau and Pesetsky had every kitchen gadget known to man. After two hours of emptying every cabinet and drawer, we bagged a mortar and pestle, as well as a "pill pulverizer" located next to Felicia's dog food.

Next, we moved to the bathrooms and found lots of meds, but no pill crushers. Likewise, we came up with nothing in the bedroom bureaus, night tables, or any of the other cabinets and drawers throughout the house. In the garage, Stan found a hammer in the toolbox and bagged it. By 11:30 p.m., we called it quits and let Pesetsky know we were done.

On the drive back to the station, we checked in with Jacoby, one of the officers who'd searched Pesetsky's office. "Came up empty," he told us. "You?"

"We've got three possibles to test for traces, but I have my doubts we'll come up with anything. Pesetksy had plenty of time to get rid of anything incriminating."

On late nights like this, Stan and I usually went to Charley's Bar and Grill, but I knew it was no fun trying to stay sober while everybody else around you was drinking. We headed for Cody's instead, an all-night diner. With its checkered floor and black, red, and chrome décor, it reminded me of my parents' collection of old *Life* magazine covers.

We loaded up on omelets and hash browns. I noticed Stan's hands were shaking slightly.

"You okay?"

"It's going to take me a while, Cait. It's like I got through the physical withdrawal in detox, but there's still that emotional pull toward booze."

I put my hand over his. "What do they say? One day, one minute at a time?"

"Yeah." He pushed his plate away. "While you finish up, mind if I step outside? I want to call my sponsor."

"Of course," I said, relieved that Stan had a sponsor and was taking this AA stuff seriously.

While he was gone, I looked around at the other late-night diners, an elderly man bent over a plate of pancakes, a group of twentyish-looking women with faces caked with heavy makeup and mascara, and a middle-aged couple who showed no signs of interest in speaking to one another. Stan and I each had our stories, stuff we were trying to work through. I couldn't help but wonder about the stories of these other folks out late on a Monday night.

When Stan came back, he looked calmer.

"Did that help?" I asked.

"Oh yeah. Tomorrow, though, I want to hit a meeting. Missed today, and I realized I can't do that."

"Understood. You know I've got your back, right?"

"I do."

———

The next morning, Stan and I drank buckets of coffee while we caught up on paperwork. I wrote up the inventory of what we'd collected from Pesetsky's house and took the items to Tony for testing.

"We're backed up here," he said. "Give me a few days."

I wasn't holding my breath. Pesetsky was not a stupid

man. I couldn't imagine him leaving anything around his house that could link him to his wife's murder. But then again, maybe it didn't occur to him that trace evidence might show up on a pill cruncher.

———

During my lunch hour, I headed to Dr. Stein's for my weekly therapy appointment. It was one of those gorgeous spring days when seemingly overnight, the landscape had turned green and lush. I breathed in the luscious scent of lilacs outside her Victorian office building.

Today, Dr. Stein wore a long dress painted with purple lilies. I loved her wardrobe and was tempted to ask her to be my personal shopper. Of course, pants suits were my go-to uniform for work. I tried to imagine being taken seriously by perps while I grilled them in a flowery dress. Stan would have a field day with that. So would the perps.

Dr. Stein greeted me warmly. I took a seat opposite her, and she said, "You look different. What's going on?"

"Overall feeling better, although we were out late last night executing a search. But Stan got out of rehab, and he apologized to me and is taking recovery seriously. I can't tell you how relieved I am. Plus, we think we caught a break on the major case we've been working on."

"Sounds very positive for events on the work front. And what's the update on your personal life?"

"Hmm… I told Chet I wanted to take a break, and he didn't try to come over last weekend—no middle-of-the-night hammering on my door, begging me to let him in."

"How did that make you feel?"

I shrugged. "Conflicted, as usual. I was proud of myself for telling him to leave me alone and not caving into his pleas for us to get together. But then there's that part of me that misses him and the whole adrenaline rush from being with him."

"Sounds pretty normal. Love affairs can feel intoxicating."

"I guess. Or addictive."

"Interesting word. In what way do you see your relationship to Chet as addictive?"

I bit my lip and paused. Finally, I said, "Well, it's a little like smoking. I used to smoke in college and in my early twenties. I knew perfectly well they were terrible for my health, and the stench got into my hair and my clothing. But I loved the feeling I got smoking a cigarette. It was hell to quit. Every once in a while, I still get a craving for one."

"Do you think Chet is not good for you, but you're addicted to the rush of being with him?"

"Definitely. I know this isn't a healthy relationship, but giving it up? I keep thinking I'm ready, but then I have my doubts I can really make a clean break. What's that expression? Like a moth to a flame?"

"That's a good analogy. And you know, the good news is that you did quit smoking, which is one of the toughest addictions to recover from. So, you should remind yourself of that. And what about Hank? Did you see him again?"

"We went out to dinner Sunday night. We talked a lot about his son and his work, as well as mine. It's still just a friendship. He hasn't even tried to kiss me, but I get the feeling he's waiting for me to say the 'someone else in my life' is gone."

"Can you see yourself doing that?"

"I don't know. I do feel attracted to Hank, but I don't have much of a track record at relationships with people who are actually available."

"Does that scare you?"

I snorted. "It does. And Hank has a seven-year-old child. He and his ex-wife split custody 50-50. He showed me a picture of his son. He's so cute, but suppose we did get involved? Talk about an insta-family. I can barely imagine being someone's committed partner, let alone a stepparent."

Dr. Stein held her hand up. "Try not to jump too far ahead. Right now, you and Hank have struck up a friendship. You enjoy one another's company, and it may or may not develop into more. As hard as it is to simply let things unfold, I think you should."

"I'm trying. I really am. This is all new territory for me."

"Have you given any more thought to identifying your own needs, apart from other people's agendas, for you?"

"I've definitely thought about it. Just keep coming up blank... You know, when I was growing up, my dad used to love this old comedy skit where a robber holds a gun on Jack Benny and says, 'Your money or your life?' And Benny replies, 'I'm thinking, I'm thinking.'"

"I remember that skit," she said with a smile. "What made you think of that?"

"Because sometimes I imagine someone coming up to me and saying, 'Someone in your life who can commit versus the exciting lover who can't?' And I'm the one saying, 'I'm thinking, I'm thinking.'"

Dr. Stein smiled. "Well, keep thinking. Remember last time when I suggested maybe it felt safer to you to stick with what you're familiar with, like your part-time relationship with Chet?"

I nodded.

"You know, I'm not usually a fan of popular self-help books, but years ago, there was a book by Susan Jeffers called *Feel the Fear and Do It Anyway.*"

I grinned. "I like the title."

"Me, too."

———

That night, Hank called. I realized I'd been waiting to hear from him and felt ridiculously glad when I did.

"I don't have my son with me this weekend. Would you

145

like to come with me to the Yale Peabody Museum of Natural History on Saturday? Science geek that I am, I think it's such a cool place."

"I haven't been there in forever. I loved it as a kid, especially the dinosaurs."

"You and my son. Jack's obsessed with dinosaurs."

"Well, then, we have something in common. I'd love to go with you, as long as you don't get too lecturey."

"Lecturey?"

"Every science teacher I've ever had goes into lecture mode when they get really excited about technical stuff."

"I'll do my best to restrain myself."

———

Stan and I focused on other cases, mostly routine, while we waited to hear about the tests on Pesetsky's pill crunchers. Friday, we got the disappointing but not unexpected news from Tony that everything came back clean. The only residue that showed up was a multi-vitamin for dogs on the pill pulverizer.

"What do you think?" I asked Stan. "Do we press for an arrest with what we've got?"

He rested his chin on his hand and hesitated. "Not sure. Your take?"

"Statistics are in our favor. The spouse is most often the guilty party. And Pesetsky had means, opportunity, and plenty of motive. How about if I write it up, we show it to Captain, and if he gives us the green light, we take it to the DA."

"Sounds like a plan."

# TWENTY-SIX

Late Friday afternoon, Captain Singleton drummed his long fingers on his desk as he flipped through the pages I'd prepared. He said nothing for several minutes, as Stan and I sat waiting. And waiting. The wall clock behind him noisily clicked off the seconds, a counterpoint to our boss's drumming.

Finally, he said, "You sure about this, O'Connor?"

I held my hands up. "I'm never 100 percent sure, but it adds up. Finding the nitroglycerin in her makeup points directly to him. And he had more than one reason to harm his wife."

Captain turned to Stan. "You agree?"

"Yeah, I do. I think it's about the insurance money to keep his company going even more than feeling pissed about his wife's cheating."

*Interesting coming from Stan, who I was pretty sure knew all about revenge fantasies due to cheating spouses.*

"Well, we've arrested on less," Captain said. He glanced at the clock. "Take it to the DA, see what he says. You'll probably have to wait until Monday, though."

He was right. Samuel Barclay told us he was on his way

out the door and to drop by Monday morning to talk. Meantime, he asked us to fax the report over, so he could give it a look beforehand. Good enough, I thought.

———

Friday night, I'd just gotten home from work, shrugged my shoes off, and poured myself a glass of wine when Chet called. "God, Caitlin, I miss you so much. We need to talk."

My stomach lurched. "I don't know. What good will that do either of us?"

"All I know is I need you. Can you come by the office tomorrow? We're backed up, and I'm putting in an extra shift. We could do lunch."

"Sorry. I have a date to go to the Museum of Natural History."

"With another guy?'

I gritted my teeth. "Like I've told you, who I spend time with doesn't concern you. And by the way, I haven't heard a thing from my mystery caller ever since we haven't been together."

"I still can't believe our relationship has anything to do with those calls."

"Think what you want, Chet."

"All I'm thinking about these days is you. I feel you slipping away," he said, his voice cracking. "I don't want to lose you."

"And you don't want to lose your marriage. And your kids. I get it."

"Tell me you don't care about me anymore, and I'll leave you alone."

Tears burned my eyes. "I... I have to go," I said, and clicked off.

I slept fitfully that night and beat myself up all Saturday morning for my inability to make a clean break from Chet. All

I'd had to say was I no longer cared in the same way, and I knew he'd leave me alone. Yet I couldn't do it. I felt hopelessly stuck, confused.

And my date with Hank didn't help matters. He was so damned nice. And handsome in his boots, jeans, and Boston Celtics sweatshirt. He made a terrific museum tour guide. I loved the Great Hall of Dinosaurs with its huge Age of Reptiles mural depicting dinosaurs in their natural habitat. The exhibit on Human Origins fascinated me as well. Hank restrained himself, but he did get excited pointing out all the details in The Age of Mammals mural.

"Do you bring your classes here?" I asked him.

"Every year. They love the Discovery Room. Nothing beats getting to touch the live snakes and other critters. My son's favorite, too." At the mention of Jack, his face clouded over.

"You miss him, don't you?"

"I do. A week is a long time not to see your kid."

"Must be tough." I wondered if our relationship would ever get to the point where I'd meet his son. I was crazy about Melissa's kids but had never imagined having my own. Until lately. Was I one of those women who gets into her late thirties and ruminates about her biological clock ticking? I didn't think so, but listening to Hank talk about Jack made me think more about what it would be like to become a parent. It was obvious he treasured every moment he got to spend with his son.

Afterward, we went down the street for Chinese at the Great Wall Restaurant where we gorged ourselves on steamed dumplings, vegetable Lo Mein, and Kung Pao Chicken. The food was delicious, the company was great, but my mind kept drifting back to my conversation with Chet the night before. Was I ready to let him go, move on? Here I was having dinner with a super nice guy I was attracted to who was actually available. What was keeping me tethered to Chet?

"You seem a little preoccupied," Hank said. "Everything okay?"

"Sorry. I guess I am. Working through some things."

He reached over and placed his warm, calloused hand over mine. "Does this have to do with the 'someone else in your life' you mentioned?"

I sighed. "Yes. It's funny," I admitted. "Even when I know something can't or won't work, I have trouble letting go of people, relationships."

"Me, too, actually. It took me a long time to get over my ex-wife. We were college sweethearts. I thought we'd be married forever, but once she realized she was never going to turn me into a more ambitious guy who made big money, she wanted out. And boy, did I resist. I didn't want to let go."

"I'm sorry. Definitely her loss."

He smiled and the crinkles around his dark eyes deepened. "Thanks for saying that." He pushed his dark curls off his forehead and held my gaze. "One thing teaching middle school has taught me is patience."

"Okay. And you mention that because..."

"Because I like you, and I'm capable of being very patient while you figure things out about your 'someone else.'"

"I'm kind of a mess right now. Not sure you should wait around."

He raised his eyebrows and grinned. "I'll take my chances."

Sunday morning, I went for a long run and then cleaned my apartment, did the laundry, and shopped for some groceries. I wasn't much of a cook, but I had a sudden hankering for some comfort food and decided to make my mom's homemade chicken noodle soup. I called Stan. "Ripley's believe it or not, I actually cooked something. You want to come over for supper?"

"I would, but I've got an AA meeting and going out afterward with my sponsor. Can I take a raincheck?"

"Sure," I said. A light rain was falling outside, and I settled down to read the *Times* while the soup simmered on the stove. I startled at the sound of heavy knocking on my door. Maybe Stan's plans had changed?

But when I peeked through my peephole, I saw Chet standing there, a bouquet of lilies, my favorite, in his hand.

# TWENTY-SEVEN

My chest tightened as I opened the door. Chet's hair was matted from the rain, and his coat looked rumpled and damp.

"What are you doing here?" I hesitated, not sure whether I should invite him in.

"I came to talk. And give you these." He handed me the flowers. "Can I come in?"

"All right, but just to talk."

He bounded by me and hung up his raincoat. "What smells so good in here?"

"Making soup. My mom's recipe." I moved into the kitchen to grab a vase for the flowers. He followed me.

"These are beautiful. Thank you," I said. "Can I get you something?"

"I wouldn't mind a beer if you've got one."

"Sure. Let me get these in water, and I'll pull a couple out."

Once I arranged the flowers and retrieved a couple of Buds from the fridge, we settled on the couch in the living room.

"You look so lovely," Chet said.

I brushed off the compliment. "What did you want to talk to me about?"

"I've decided. I can't stay married to Marian and be in love with someone else. I want us to be together. Really together. I finally talked to Marian, told her how I was feeling. We've agreed to separate at the end of the school year."

My heart pounded. "But... but what about your kids?"

"We'll work it out. I'll stay in their lives as much as I can. But I can't go on living a lie. It's not fair to anyone. And I've been so miserable, not seeing you, being with you."

I searched his face—his perfectly sculpted cheekbones and sky-blue eyes, and the tiny scar above his right eye from a high school soccer collision. My thoughts tripped over one another. Was this for real? Could I trust him? And did I really want to break up someone's marriage?

"This is a big decision, Chet. Just a few weeks ago, you ended things with me. Now you're saying you want me and not your marriage. I think you need to take some time to make sure this is really what you want."

He pounded his fist into the couch arm rest. "God damn it, Caitlin. I know what I want. It's you." He pulled me toward him and spread a line of kisses up my neck to my ear, my cheek, and finally my mouth.

I felt the familiar longing that began deep in my groin and worked its way up through my entire body.

He reached his hand inside my shirt and bra, and found my breast, grazing my nipple, which grew taut beneath his touch. "Tell me you don't want this, don't want me."

"I can't."

Chet left around eight. We'd made love, eaten soup, and made love again. As I lay in bed that night, I thought about how much I craved his touch, wanted to believe Chet and I could have a happily ever after. He'd maneuvered his way back into my bed. Once again, we were lovers. Once again, he'd gone home to his wife. And when the end of the school year came, would he really leave her?

Monday morning, Stan and I headed over to the DA's office. Samuel Barclay's assistant, a fiftyish-looking woman with a long face and a beehive jet-black hairdo, ushered us into his office. He greeted us with his customary booming voice. A short, skinny guy, he must figure he needed to turn up his speaking volume to disabuse anyone of the notion that he could be pushed around.

He took his seat behind an enormous mahogany desk covered with stacks of paper, and we sat down on the other side. Awards, plaques, and photographs of him with the mayor and a couple of senators covered his walls. He wanted everyone who came to see him to know he, a working-class kid from Pittsburgh, had made it bigtime.

He picked up the report I'd faxed him. "Looks like you've done your homework," he said. "Ingenious way to knock off your wife. I just hope you've got this right. Pesetsky's a bigwig in the arts here. If this case falls apart, we're going to catch major shit. You know I don't like surprises, especially near an election. This witness who saw him enter her dressing room that morning—You think he's a lock?"

"He's not going to be thrilled about testifying. Pesetsky's his boss, and he needs the job. But he doesn't strike me as someone who'd refuse a subpoena." A sliver of guilt wove its way up my chest. We hadn't mentioned that Frederick Pesetsky had also been seen that morning going into Lydia Miseau's dressing room. It was possible he'd stolen his dad's nitroglycerin to do away with his stepmother. I just didn't think it was likely. No point in muddying the waters when we were almost sure we had the right guy.

Barclay tossed the report on his desk and clasped his hands beneath his chin. His gaze moved from me to Stan. "You on board with this, Bisso?"

"I'm in," Stan said. "Pesetsky had a lot to gain from his wife's death."

"Okay, then." Barclay pushed his intercom button. "Gladys, prepare a warrant for the arrest of Victor Pesetsky. First degree murder of Lydia Miseau."

———

"You can't be serious!" Pesetsky said, when we interrupted his rehearsal that afternoon to arrest him. Dancers dripping in perspiration stood frozen, staring at us as though we were alien invaders in their universe.

Except for Muriel Gaston, who rushed forward to confront us. She pulled up inches from me and pointed a finger at my chest. "You are making a terrible mistake. Victor would never have hurt Lydia."

"Ma'am, we need you to step aside," I said, as Stan handcuffed Victor.

"What can I do?" she screamed at Victor.

"Get Frederick. Tell him to look after Felicia, Lydia's, our, I mean my dog until I'm home. And have him call my attorney." Victor turned to me. "This is ridiculous! You're going to be very sorry for this."

I didn't respond as we led him out the door.

———

I was sure Pesetsky wasn't enjoying his night in jail. My night wasn't so hot either. Another call, this time at 4 a.m., from my creepy stalker who told me in the usual distorted voice that I was "a shit of a human being" who'd get what I deserved. "Soon."

I slammed down the phone and paced around my apartment. At this point, I was more annoyed than freaked out by these stupid calls that came like clockwork after I'd been with Chet. But if Marian was behind these calls, and now she and Chet had agreed to separate, what was the point? Revenge? Making my life as miserable as she blamed me for making hers? I had no idea.

All I knew was I felt way too wired to go back to sleep. I poured myself a glass of wine and curled up on the couch. I turned on the TV and scrolled past a cooking show, one on how to make millions flipping real estate, and a true crime episode about a man accused of killing his wife. Naturally, he got convicted, and all loose ends were neatly tied up by the time the credits were rolling. If only real life "true crime" cases were that neat and easy.

------

Pesetsky's attorney Margolis knew his stuff. By the next morning, Pesetsky had posted a hefty bond and was released pending trial. Meantime, I fielded dozens of calls from the media who didn't like my "No comment" and "Our investigation is continuing" statements.

------

The news commentators had a field day speculating about the relationship between Pesetsky and Miseau, and what might have driven the artistic director to murder his wife, the star of his company.

By the time I got to my lunchtime Tuesday therapy appointment with Dr. Stein, I felt unmoored by the media hounding, not to mention what was going on in my personal life.

She greeted me warmly. "I gather you've been busy."

"Too busy. It's a regular media circus."

"Are you feeling pleased, though, about having made an arrest?"

I sighed. "I guess. I just hope we're right. When a case is entirely circumstantial, I always have that seed of doubt."

She nodded. "And what else has been going on for you?"

I hung my head. "You probably don't want to know," I mumbled.

"Try me."

I filled her in on the events of the weekend—Hank telling me he liked me and planned to be patient, followed by Chet's dramatic announcement that he and his wife were separating and my falling back into bed with him.

"Sounds like quite a weekend," she said, pushing her tortoise-shelled glasses up her nose. "How do you feel about all this?"

"Confused, as usual. I had such a nice time with Hank, and then the next day, Chet tells me he and his wife are splitting, and he wants to be with me. I feel like a wad of silly putty being pulled in a million directions—well, at least two, anyway. Oh, and I got another creepy call last night. Those come every time right after I've been with Chet."

"Sounds like a lot of pressure on you right now."

"It is. Some days, I just want to crawl under the covers and not come out."

Dr. Stein smiled. "I think we all feel that way sometimes. But tell me, assuming he does separate from his wife, can you visualize yourself with Chet on a more fulltime basis?"

"I don't know. I never wanted to be a homewrecker. I saw what my friend Melissa went through when her parents divorced, and I feel so guilty thinking about putting Chet's kids through that. And if these calls are coming from his wife, she's obviously out to hurt me—even if it's just to scare me. But I've been in love with this man for a long time. And I'm starting to feel I deserve more than a few stolen hours with a parttime lover."

"And do you trust Chet? That he's telling you the truth? He's really going to leave his wife and be with you?"

I gazed at her solemnly. "As my dad used to say, 'That's the $64,000 question.'"

"And one worth finding the answer to. I'm not telling you anything you don't know when I say that healthy relationships are based on trust and honest communication. And by the way, I want to commend you for being honest with Hank —that this other relationship exists and you're still trying to figure things out."

I dug my nails into my palms. "Yeah, but I feel guilty—like maybe I'm stringing him along while I see if this future with Chet is going to pan out."

"As long as you're upfront with him, it's his choice as to whether he wants to continue spending time with you, knowing that things may never progress beyond friendship."

"I guess. It's just, he's such a good guy, and I don't want to hurt him. He's barely gotten over his divorce."

"Sometimes we have to trust our gut feelings."

"And that's the problem. My gut is sending me way too many mixed messages."

———

After my appointment with Dr. Stein, I headed over to Ballet Études to talk to Gus. When I came in, Dora, whose hair remained spiked into a dozen purple, green, and orange corn rows, glared at me. "I can't believe you arrested Victor," she said.

"Just doing my job. Is Gus around?"

She sniffed. "He's here—no idea exactly where."

I found him mopping the backstage area. When he saw me, he frowned—one more person who didn't look happy that I'd dropped by.

"Hey Gus, I wanted to tell you we're going to need to take a deposition from you about seeing Victor Pesetsky entering Ms. Miseau's dressing room the morning she died."

"Like I told you, Detective, Victor always brought her flowers when a show was about to go up. That's all he was doing, and that's all I seen." His eyes were doing that darting around thing again.

"All I'm asking for, Gus, is that you tell what you witnessed—nothing more. We'll subpoena you. Mr. Pesetsky will understand that you had no choice but to answer our questions."

His face contorted. "I'm sorry I ever told you about him delivering the flowers. Victor wouldn't have hurt Lydia."

"I'm just doing my job, Gus."

"Yeah, okay. But you gotta understand. I need to keep my job."

"Hopefully, that won't be an issue."

And as I walked away, I hoped it wouldn't be. I remembered how awful my mom had looked in the weeks after Dad had been diagnosed. I knew Gus's wife was fighting cancer, and I recognized the familiar lines of fatigue and worry etched on his face.

That night, Hank called and said what a wonderful time he'd had with me on Saturday. "And I didn't realize I was hanging out with a celebrity. You're all over the papers with news about your arrest of that ballet director."

"It's been a little crazy," I admitted.

"I recommend a quiet, relaxing evening out," he said. "I've got Jack this week, but how about dinner on Sunday night? There's a new Mexican place I'd love to try."

I hesitated. Finally, I said, "Hank, I want to be really honest with you. The 'someone else' I told you about is still in my life. I may never be able to offer you more than friendship."

He heaved an audible sigh. "I do believe this has come up

159

before. Look Caitlin, I like you. I like spending time with you. And if it's never going to move beyond that, well, so be it."

"I don't want to lead you on."

"You're not. How about if I pick you up around seven on Sunday?"

"You're on."

# TWENTY-EIGHT

A cross town, Gus paced back and forth in his tiny living room. He thought about the way all those bad guys talked on Mary's crime shows. Gruff, sure of themselves, not taking "no" for an answer. He was no actor. It had been hard enough the first time. But when he thought about his Mary, wasting away little by little, he knew he had to do it.

His fingers shook as he put in the call to his mark.

"Going to need another $5,000," he said in the gruffest voice he could muster.

"I don't know if I can come up with that."

"I don't think you've got much of a choice." He wiped perspiration off his brow. "I know you wouldn't want me going to the police and telling them what I seen."

"I need some time."

"Tell you what—I'll give you until tomorrow night to lay your hands on another $5,000. Same place. Now that it's staying light longer, let's make it 10 p.m. this time."

Gus didn't wait for an answer. He clicked off and went to check on Mary.

# TWENTY-NINE

The call came in shortly after midnight. Ernie Levine, a patrol officer making a drive-through around the abandoned warehouse that had once been the Lehman Brothers Engraving Factory, had discovered the city's most recent homicide victim sprawled inside his vehicle, an ancient rusted out Chevy. Gus Mikowski had been shot in the chest three times.

My stomach lurched at the news. "Shit," I said to Ernie. "That's our witness in the Miseau murder case."

"Huh. Too bad. It doesn't look like a robbery. Guy still had his wallet on him."

"On my way. Have you called the forensics guys and the medical examiner?"

"Yeah."

"Good. Rope off the area, and don't touch anything."

"I know the drill, Detective," he said, sounding irritated.

Great. All I needed was one more uniform, thinking I was one of those arrogant suits—worse yet, a woman. "Of course," I said. "Thanks."

On the drive over, I called Stan. He didn't sound right. His words had that slurred quality I recognized. I gripped the steering wheel and prayed that the way he sounded came from being woken from a deep sleep and not because he'd relapsed. He'd been doing so well.

"Are you okay?" I asked.

"Had a bad night. JoAnne called. Wanted to tell me that she's having a baby before I heard it from anybody else. Said she wanted me to be happy for her in her 'wonderful new life.'"

"I take it the daddy is that hot shot VP from her company?"

His voice sounded even wobblier as he said, "Oh yeah, the one and only Arnold Fitzhugh. They pushed the wedding date up for obvious reasons."

"I'm so sorry, Stan. I know it hurts."

He sighed. "I broke down and tossed a few back after she called. I don't want you to worry. I've already called my sponsor. He's coming over."

"I'm glad you called him. Look, I can handle this by myself tonight. You good to come in tomorrow?"

"Yeah. Are you going to tell Captain about this?'

"That's up to you. If it happens again, I'll have to."

———

By the time I got to the warehouse property, the forensics guys were in full swing combing the scene and taking pictures. I found Chet bent over the body. My heart hammered in my chest as I moved toward him. "Hey," I said. "What's it look like?"

He straightened and turned to face me. "Don't think he's been dead for long—two, three hours at the most. No defensive wounds on his hands. I don't think he had any idea the shooter was going to open fire on him."

"The vic is Gus Mikowski, the guy who was going to testify in the Miseau case."

"You think this is connected?"

"No idea. But it sure seems like a mighty big coincidence."

He touched my arm. "You'll figure it out. I'll give you a call as soon as I know anything more, okay?"

I nodded and walked away, amazed at how Chet's touch still set off something warm and tingly inside me.

———

Back in my car, I logged into the Motor Vehicle Bureau records and got Gus's address. This was my least favorite part of the job, but someone had to tell Gus's wife that her husband was dead.

Twenty minutes later, I pulled up to a small brick home in a neighborhood that had seen better days. It was an apartment in a house that had been turned into a rental with two apartments. The place featured two doorbells, and I pressed the one labeled Mikowski. A painfully thin woman in a faded bathrobe opened the door a crack.

"I'm Detective O'Connor," I said, flashing my badge. "May I come in?"

She ushered me in and said, "My husband—I just realized he's not here."

"Can we sit down?"

"Of course." She pushed some newspapers aside and gestured for me to take a seat on the threadbare couch. Her pale, drawn face searched mine. "Do you know where Gus is?"

"I'm afraid I have bad news. Earlier this evening, your husband was shot and killed. An officer found him in his vehicle in the parking lot behind the old Lehman Brothers Engraving Factory."

She gasped and brought her spindly hand to her mouth. "No!" she wailed. "No! My Gus gone? He's all I have in the world." She buried her face in her hands and sobbed.

"I'm so sorry. Let me get you some water."

I moved toward the back of her flat and found the kitchen. With its puckered linoleum floor, it looked like it hadn't been updated since the 1970s. But it was neat as a pin. I fished out a jelly glass and quickly filled it with water.

When I brought it out to her, her sobs had quieted. Her hands shook as she raised the glass up to her mouth for a tentative sip before setting it down on the plywood coffee table. "I want to see him," she said.

"Yes, of course. We'll need you to make a positive identification. The medical examiner will be conducting an autopsy at the city morgue. Do you want me to take you down there tomorrow?"

"Yes. I don't drive," she said. "But I don't understand. Why would anyone shoot my Gus? He doesn't have an enemy in the world. And what was he doing there?"

"I don't know. I was hoping you might have some idea."

She shook her head. "I have no idea. I've been sick, and I went to bed early. I had no idea he'd gone out."

"Did he mention anything to you about having to testify in the case against Victor Pesetsky?"

Her mouth gaped open. "No. He always said Mr. Pesetsky was a fine man, a good boss. Why would Gus have testified against him?"

"He told me that he'd observed Pesetsky entering Lydia Miseau's empty dressing room the morning she died to deliver some flowers."

"Gus never said a word about that. I'm sorry."

"Did you notice anything that struck you as odd or different in recent weeks?"

Her reddened eyes widened. "There was something. I don't get out much anymore, so I pay all our bills online. Last week, I was shocked to find a deposit I didn't recognize in our checking account. It was a lot of money, $5,000. When I asked Gus about it, he told me it was a loan from one of the ballet company's benefactors who'd heard about my illness and wanted to help."

"Did he say who?"

"No. He didn't seem to want to talk about it. He knows I don't like feeling like a charity case. But my Gus was determined to find the money to pay for this experimental treatment for my cancer. Our insurance doesn't cover it."

"So, will the $5,000 be enough?"

"It's going to be a lot more than that. But at least we had enough to pay for the first installment." She paused, and a fresh set of tears dripped down her face. "I wanted to call hospice, let go. But Gus insisted we had to try everything possible, said he'd find the money somehow. With him gone, I'm not sure I even want to go through one more treatment. What's the point?"

I swallowed hard. "Not something you should decide right now when you're dealing with such upsetting news."

She sniffed and swiped a matted handkerchief across her cheeks. "I suppose you're right."

"May I have your permission to access your bank records?"

She looked startled. "I suppose. We bank at Chase. I can call them tomorrow. But what are you saying? That the $5,000 might have something to do with Gus's getting shot?"

"It's something I want to check out. Meantime, is there anyone I can call who could come and be with you?"

"I don't have any family here. Maybe my upstairs neighbor, Beth? We've gotten pretty friendly. Sometimes she picks up my medications for me." She handed me the phone and gave me the number.

I briefly explained the situation to Beth, and her sleepy voice immediately sharpened. "Oh my God, I'll be right there." A gray-haired woman with a kind, pock-marked face arrived moments later, wearing a hot pink housecoat and lavender fluffy slippers. She immediately took her neighbor in her arms. "Oh Mary, my poor, poor girl. I'm so sorry," she said, over and over.

I stood up to go. "I'm going to leave my card here."

Mary Mikowski mumbled her thanks.

"I'll call tomorrow about going to the morgue."

"All right," she said.

Beth jumped up. "Going to make us some tea," she announced as I slipped out the door.

———

By the next morning, I was running on fumes. I couldn't get the picture of Mary Mikowski's grief-stricken face out of my mind. The thing about homicide is that there's never just one victim. The loved ones left behind are the real sufferers.

Stan staggered in around nine. "My sponsor stayed with me last night. He says this happens a lot early in recovery, but it's really good I called him right away. I think I'm going to be okay, get back on track."

"Hope so," I said. "You look like hell."

"You, too. Did you have to tell the vic's wife?"

"Yup. Pretty awful. She's really sick, and now this."

"She have any ideas what he was doing there?"

"No, but she told me something interesting. Gus deposited $5,000 into their account a few days ago. Said it was a loan from one of the ballet company's benefactors to help pay for her cancer treatment."

Stan's eyebrows lifted high on his forehead. "Are you thinking what I'm thinking?"

I nodded. "Every time I talked to Gus, he looked so nervous. I'm wondering if he saw more than he told me and was squeezing somebody."

"Pesetsky's out on bail. We should definitely find out what he was doing last night," Stan said.

"Bingo."

Three hours later, we'd checked out Pesetsky's alibi, and damn if it didn't appear to be ironclad. He'd attended an emergency board meeting of the company to discuss next steps, given the court case against him. The meeting didn't break up until well after ten, and Pesetsky had gone out for drinks afterward at Tavern on State with Frederick along with two of his biggest board supporters. The bartender confirmed that the group didn't leave until close to one a.m., well past the time Ernie Levine had discovered Gus's body.

A bad feeling about this edged its way into the pit of my stomach. If Gus had been shaking someone down about Miseau's murder, and it wasn't Pesetsky, then who? I didn't even want to think about the possibility we'd arrested the wrong man. My ass would be hung out to dry by Captain Singleton, not to mention the DA.

Maybe there was another explanation. But why would Gus have driven to the parking lot behind an abandoned warehouse? And why would someone shoot him? I'd checked his record. Totally clean. No evidence of any wrongdoing. Ever. But I knew from experience that when perfectly pleasant law-abiding citizens are desperate enough, they're capable of doing desperate things. And Gus had been determined to get the money for his wife's treatment.

Stan was at an AA meeting, and I was about to make a coffee run when Muriel Gaston walked into the station and strode toward me. With her hair down, she looked impossibly young. And nervous. Her lips twitched, and she avoided my gaze. "I'm here to make a statement," she said.

*Now what?* "Maybe you'd better sit down." I led her over to my desk and guided her into a chair opposite mine. "What is this about?"

"You need to drop the charges against Victor. He did not kill Lydia. I did."

My jaw dropped somewhere around my breastbone. "Are

you telling me you wish to make a confession that you killed Lydia?"

"Yes." Her mouth trembled. She gazed down at her tightly clasped hands.

I leaned forward. "I must advise you to retain the services of an attorney."

"I don't need an attorney. I'm here to confess. Just do that thing you do, you know, where you say the warnings."

"You want me to Mirandize you?"

"Yes, that's it. I forgot what it's called for a minute."

"Okay then." I ran through Miranda and then said, "Why don't you tell me what happened?"

Her face scrunched up in concentration. "Well, you know, I grabbed some nitroglycerin from Victor's office when he was out, and then I put some in Lydia's makeup."

"Where in Victor's office did you find the nitroglycerin?"

"Uh… you know, in his desk."

"Where in his desk?"

She shifted in her seat. "Uh… I don't remember exactly. I was in a hurry."

"You think it was his top drawer?"

"I guess. Like I said, I was in a hurry."

Victor kept his meds in his bottom drawer. I was almost sure she was lying. But why? "Okay, so then what did you do?"

"Well, you know, I waited until Lydia wasn't in there, and I put the medication in her makeup."

"How did you do that?"

"Just… you know, mixed it in there."

"And how did you prepare it?"

"Just… got it ready," she said, evasively.

*She has no idea.* "And where did you get the idea that this would be a good way to kill her?"

This question seemed to stump her. "I don't know. I must have read about it somewhere."

"Where?"

Her shoulders lifted. "I don't know. I read a lot of things."

I leaned forward. "And you didn't worry that you'd be implicating Victor?"

Her eyes widened. "No, of course not. I would never hurt Victor. I wouldn't hurt any..." She paused, as if she'd just realized what she was about to say. "I mean, I only wanted to hurt Lydia—not anyone else."

"And why was that?"

"She took Paul away from me. She refused to retire, and frankly, I was tired of waiting around for my chance to become the company's principal dancer. Every year, she'd say she was going to hang it up, and then she'd change her mind."

*Well, that rang true. But her confession? Not a chance.*

"And you'd be willing to take a lie detector test?"

She shook her head. "I don't have to, do I? Can't you just take my word for it? I did it, okay? You can let Victor go now."

I sat back in my chair and studied her. "Muriel, I'm not sure what you think you're doing, but I don't believe you. You can't remember where Victor kept his nitroglycerin, you can't recall how you knew about using it to kill Lydia, and you don't really know what you did to get the medication ready to put into her makeup. What game are you playing here?"

Her face crumpled. "It's not a game! Don't you see? All you have is a pile of circumstantial evidence. You don't have a witness! Any of us could have killed Lydia."

"So let me get this straight. You thought if you confessed, you'd get Victor off, save the company, and you'd never get convicted because you could rescind your confession, and there'd always be reasonable doubt—any of you who had a reason to resent Lydia could have done it. Am I getting warm here?"

Tears sprang into her eyes and dripped down her face. "I was just trying to help. I know Victor. He couldn't have done this. You're making a huge mistake."

I sighed. "That may be. We'll have to let the court decide. But making a false confession is not helping. I suggest you go home before I decide to charge you with obstruction of justice."

Muriel grabbed her dance bag, stood up, and hauled herself to standing. She glared down at me. "You wait and see, Detective. You'll be very sorry that you arrested the wrong person."

She lifted her head above her swan-like neck and stalked out. I watched her go and a shiver passed through me. She seemed so damned sure we'd gotten this all wrong. And our witness who'd seen Victor enter Lydia's dressing room that morning was dead.

# THIRTY

When Stan came back from his meeting, I filled him in on Muriel's attempted confession.

His mouth dropped open. "God, she's either a loony-tune or really gutsy."

"Maybe a little of both. My guess is she thinks her confession could poke holes in our case and any jury would conclude reasonable doubt that she'd offed her rival. Too many folks around with means, motive, and opportunity."

He scratched his head. "But why confess to something you didn't do? Risk ruining your own life?"

"Think about it. Victor goes down for this, and most likely, the company folds. There goes her chance to become its star. So, if she can make the case that anybody could have killed Lydia, she gets herself off. And Victor."

His eyebrows knitted together. "In a crazy way, that makes sense. But what a gamble. Good thing she turned out to be a lousy liar."

"No kidding."

An hour later, I called Chet for an update and to let him know I'd be bringing Mary over to make a positive ID that afternoon.

"Looks like he was shot with a 38. My guess would be close range. Died instantly."

"Okay. Going to bring his wife over. Two good?"

"Sure. I've got a meeting, but Burt can help you." He lowered his voice. "The other night was really special. I'm excited about our future."

He sounded so sincere. So why didn't I fully believe him? "One day at a time," I said.

"You're starting to sound like someone in AA, Cait."

"Well, Stan and I hang out a lot."

He laughed, "I can tell."

———

I picked Mary up around 1:30 p.m.. She wore a faded navy dress that hung on her bony frame. The poor woman was literally wasting away.

"Will they let me touch him?' she asked.

"No. I'm sorry. You'll only get to view him behind a glass partition."

"I... I wanted to give him a final kiss goodbye," she said, her voice cracking.

"Maybe after they release the body, you'll be able to."

"I've been racking my brain about who could have done this. Everyone liked my Gus."

"I promise you we're going to do a thorough investigation. Did you have a chance to call your bank, by the way?"

"Totally forgot. I'll call right now. She pulled an old flip-top cell phone out of her bag and spoke to the bank manager, Mr. Clarington. She explained my request and listened for a moment. "He wants to talk to you."

I grabbed the phone. "Lieutenant O'Connor," I said. "As Mrs. Mikowski told you, she's given us permission to examine her recent bank records from the joint accounts she held with her late husband."

Mr. Clarington insisted I come down and show him my badge to retrieve the records. "I'm sure you can understand we have to take every precaution to protect our clients' privacy."

"I do. And I'm sure you can understand that this is a homicide investigation."

———

The morgue, as usual, was chilly and smelled of death and formalin. Mary visibly trembled as we stood behind the glass partition, and Burt, one of the autopsy technicians, wheeled a stainless-steel table carrying the sheet-covered body into the viewing area.

"Are you ready?" he said through the intercom.

Mary nodded, and he pulled the sheet off the bald, lifeless head of Gus Mikowski.

She wailed and collapsed in my arms. "Oh, my Gus, my Gus. I kept hoping it was all a terrible mistake."

I tightened my arms around her. "I can't tell you how sorry I am." I silently waved to Burt who quickly replaced the sheet over Gus's head. I led Mary down the hall and back to the car.

———

When I dropped Mary off, Beth must have been waiting. Her door shot open, and she rushed downstairs to be with her neighbor. I promised to check in on Mary soon and felt relieved that Beth was around to offer her support and comfort.

I dropped by the bank, picked up Mary and Gus's bank records, and headed back to the station where I studied the bank printouts. It was clear Gus and Mary had exhausted their savings and Gus's salary barely covered their monthly bills.

The $5,000 cash deposit stood out as the largest amount Gus had ever put into their account.

I put in a call to Frederick Pesetsky whose tone was decidedly frosty when I identified myself. "What do you want now, Detective?"

"As you may or may not be aware, your head custodian, Gus Mikowski, was found shot dead last night."

He gasped. "Gus? Oh, no. I didn't know. How awful. Gus has worked with us for years. What happened?"

"That's what we're trying to figure out. I need a list from you of the company's major benefactors."

"Why in the world would you need that?"

"Routine follow-up. Gus told his wife he'd gotten a generous loan from a big company supporter to help with her cancer treatment. Were you aware of anything about that?"

"No. I can't imagine any of our benefactors even knew Gus."

"Did you, by any chance, loan him money?"

"No. And I manage my father's money, and I would have known if he'd loaned Gus anything."

"Okay—well, if you can fax me over a list of your major donors, the ones who could afford to make a $5,000 loan to Gus, that would be very helpful."

"Look, you're not going to accuse them of anything, are you? We can't afford to alienate any of our patrons. Surely you understand."

"I do. And no, all we want is verification of Gus's story that he received the loan."

"All right then. And so you know, Margolis is arranging for my father to take a lie detector test. He did not kill Lydia."

"Too bad those aren't legally admissible. But thanks for your help on Gus's case." I gave him our fax number.

"Goodbye, Detective," he said curtly, and clicked off.

Bubbles of anxiety bounced around in my gut. Even though results of lie detector tests couldn't be used in court, the fact that Victor Pesetsky was happy to take one indicated a level of confidence in his innocence that didn't bode well for our case. And if he passed the test, his attorney would undoubtedly leak the results to the media. Not good. So not good.

———

After Stan returned from his AA meeting, I filled him in on my talk with the younger Pesetsky. "I don't like that Victor is so willing to take a lie detector test," I admitted.

Stan's face scrunched up. "Me neither. But some folks figure they can beat the test, even when they're guilty as sin."

While we were talking, the fax came in from the younger Pesetsky listing dozens of benefactors who might have loaned Gus money. Stan and I divided up the names and began phoning the company's well-to-do supporters. Around six, we sent out for pizza and continued making calls. By 9 p.m., we gave up for the night. We'd come up with absolutely nothing. Only a couple of the ballet patrons we talked to even knew who Gus was, and none reported loaning him money.

I rubbed my temple and pulled out some Advil for a bitch of a headache that had come on about an hour into our phone marathon. "What's your take on this?"

"Gus told a story he thought his wife would buy as to where he got the money. He was trying to make a deal that went bad."

"Yeah. I figure extortion, and the vic didn't want to pay any more for Gus's silence. Ten to one, this was connected to Miseau's murder. Frederick could be trying to protect his dad —or himself, for that matter. I want to subpoena both of their bank records to see if there are any notable withdrawals. Sure, they have alibis for the shooting, but that doesn't mean one or both of them didn't pay somebody to take care of Gus."

"Good idea," Stan said.

I shrugged. "Truthfully, it's a long shot. I can't picture Victor or Frederick having the foggiest idea how to contact a hitman."

"So maybe Gus had the goods on someone else? You're thinking our case is going to blow up?"

"It's a definite possibility. How do you feel about you and me going back to handing out parking tickets?"

Stan groaned. "Don't say that to a guy trying to stay sober."

"Sorry." And I was.

———

The next day, Stan and I managed to track down the final benefactors we hadn't been able to reach the night before. We came up empty. No one had loaned money to Gus, although like the donors we'd talked to previously, they were very sorry to hear about his murder. I was tempted to suggest they express their sympathy by donating for Mary Mikowski's treatment, but I knew it wasn't my place to ask.

Meantime, Judge Randolph signed off on our subpoenas for the Pesetsky's bank records. Once again, we struck out. We learned that father and son had a lot in common. They enjoyed fine dining and shopping for antiques and artwork. But they hadn't withdrawn any large amounts of cash from their accounts in the last several weeks.

"I don't like the way this is smelling," I told Stan.

"Me neither."

———

By the end of the week, I was in a total funk. I still had no idea who'd offed Gus. But I was increasingly certain he'd been less than forthcoming about what he knew about Miseau's murder.

Why else would he have looked so nervous every time I talked to him?

And then there was Chet, who hadn't called for days. If he and his wife had really agreed to separate, wouldn't he be freer to see me, talk to me?

Saturday morning, I went for a long run. Forsythia was out in full bloom, and I passed lots of fellow joggers and walkers enjoying the spring weather. I breathed in the scent of freshly mowed grass. The season of hope and new beginnings, I thought. But not for poor Mary Mikowski. And probably not for me.

When I got home, I poured a huge glass of OJ and fixed myself some cinnamon toast and coffee. I wondered what Chet was up to today with his supposedly about-to-be splintered family. I suddenly had the overwhelming desire to find out.

I knew where he lived. Out of morbid curiosity, I'd even driven by his colonial house in one of Hamden's prosperous subdivisions a couple of times. But I'd never been tempted to spy on him and his family.

Until now. I drove to a spot down the block from his house and parked. With my binoculars, I could get a clear view of anyone coming in or out of his house, but I was far enough away that I doubted he or his family members would notice me.

It had been a while since I'd done a stake-out. I'd forgotten how deadly dull they could be. Hour after hour of sitting there, watching for anything that might or might not happen.

I studied their house. It looked like something straight out of a family sitcom with its cheerful hanging plants on the wrap-around porch, manicured lawn, and basketball goal in the driveway. Kids rode up and down the street on scooters and bikes, watchful parents keeping them in view.

It was nearly lunchtime when Chet emerged with his family. Their seven-year-old, Benjy, pulled a shiny red wagon which carried his little sister, as well as a large wicker basket. My guess was they were headed to the park a couple of blocks away for a picnic.

Chet's arm was slung around Marian, and they were talking and laughing. At one point, their little caravan came to a stop, as Benjy knelt down to tie his shoe. That's when I noticed the change in Marian's appearance. A definite bump protruded from her middle. She absently patted it, and Chet put his hand over hers and gave her a quick kiss.

My heart sank to my knees. Chet had been lying through his teeth. His wife was pregnant, and this family looked to be in no danger of coming apart.

The only person coming apart was me.

# THIRTY-ONE

I don't know how I managed to drive, my eyes nearly swollen shut from crying. Once I got home, I locked myself in my apartment and lay on the couch with the rose-colored afghan my grandma had made me for my twelfth birthday. I went through a large box of Kleenex and got up only to pee and fix myself endless cups of tea.

I didn't want to talk to anybody. I played my favorite B.B. King blues for hours and let myself wallow in grief. I didn't pick up calls from Melissa, my mom, or Stan—just texted them to say I "must have come down with something" and would phone as soon as I felt better. I texted the same message to Hank and asked for a raincheck on our Sunday night dinner date.

Chet left three voicemails late Saturday night, saying he wanted to see me. I didn't respond. I was so done playing his game.

And that's what it had been, one long game in which I played the part of the chump. Why had I ever thought he really cared about me? Needed me for anything more than steamy illicit sex? What was he planning to tell me when the school year ended, and his supposed separation from his wife never happened?

I clutched my stomach. What hurt the most was knowing that I'd bought into a fantasy. Chet didn't love me. He'd manipulated me, used me.

And was I any better than he was? Hadn't I used him to feel cared about without having to put in the investment and work involved in a real relationship?

When I wasn't beating myself up or weeping over the death of the dream starring Chet and me riding off into the sunset, I kept coming back to the question of why he'd lied to me about splitting from Marian. I finally decided it was a calculated move on his part to reel me back in as his extra-marital fuck buddy. What had he said? "I feel you slipping away." And I had been—going out with Hank, getting into therapy, telling Chet we should take a break.

By Sunday night, I told myself that at least I had some clarity. I'd been so conflicted and confused about my feelings for this man who claimed to love me. Now who he was and what we'd had, or hadn't had, was clear. Nothing to do but heat up some chicken noodle soup and lay my clothes out for the next day.

―――――

"Feeling better?" Stan asked when I slid into my office chair Monday morning.

"A little bit. How was your weekend?"

"Not bad. My sister came in from Jersey, and we had a big family dinner yesterday. Mom's in heaven because my sister's expecting."

At the mention of pregnancy, my brain flashed on the image of Marian patting her stomach. I pushed it away. "That's nice, Stan. No relapses?"

"Nope. Too busy going to meetings. You know what they say—one-a-day until it works."

"You look good." And he did. His eyes were brighter, clearer.

"Working on it. Joey wants to fix me up on a date next weekend. Someone he works with. Don't know if I'm ready."

"You're ready."

"I'm thinking about it. What's going on with you and lover-boy?"

I held my hand up. "Don't ask."

We spent the day catching up on paperwork and helping Vince interview three witnesses to a hit-and-run. The fourteen-year-old victim was expected to survive, but he'd sustained a traumatic brain injury. The poor kid would never be the same. Neither would his parents.

Late that afternoon, we got a surprise visit from Victor Pesetsky and his attorney.

"We need to talk," Pesetsky said.

We took them to a conference room and Margolis shoved a report in front of me. I glanced down and skimmed the results of Pesetsky's lie detector test. "Looks like you passed with flying colors. You do understand, as I told your son, that these results are not legally admissible."

Victor straightened the fedora that topped his head and looked down his long aquiline nose at me. "Perhaps not, but I thought you should be aware of them. I have every intention of fighting your false arrest of me. I did not harm my wife, and it's your job to find out who did."

Margolis spoke up then. "Have you considered that the murder of Gus Mikowski could be connected to this case?"

"I can assure you that we are investigating every possible angle. That's all I can say right now."

"Well, all I can say is that you'd better be doing a thorough investigation and not trying to railroad my client," Margolis said.

"That's not how we operate," Stan said. "All we want is justice for Lydia Miseau, as well as Gus Mikowski."

Pesetsky sniffed. "I certainly hope so. I had nothing to do with either death. Gus worked for us faithfully for more than a decade. As a matter of fact, Frederick plans to solicit donations from everyone associated with Ballet Études to help Gus's wife, who's been quite ill."

"That sounds like a wonderful way to honor his memory," I said. "Tell Frederick I'd like to make a donation as well. And rest assured we plan to do everything we can to track down his killer."

Margolis stood up and gestured to Pesetsky to join him. "We'll be in touch." Then he couldn't resist one final parting shot. "Let's hope you do a better job of investigating this latest homicide than you've done for Lydia Miseau."

*Ouch.*

Stan turned to me after they left. "Why do I feel like we're not their favorite people?"

"Can't imagine."

# THIRTY-TWO

Gerald Gladstone, Sarah Pesetsky's father, hobbled down the hallway to retrieve a book on Jackson Pollock from his study when he overheard his daughter talking on the phone, apparently to his personal physician. He paused and leaned heavily on his cane. His mouth hung open in disbelief. The moment she clicked off, he moved into the den where Sarah sat picking at a nail.

"Why on earth would you say such a thing to Dr. Hughes?" he asked. "You owe me an explanation."

Her eyes surveyed him as though he were an inconvenience she needed to correct. "I'm sorry you had to hear that, Dad. But memory loss at your age... well, it's natural. Your doctor was very understanding."

She stood up, walked over to him, and patted his arm.

He flicked it away. "I don't know what you're up to, Sarah, but I intend to find out." He turned around and limped out of the room.

# THIRTY-THREE

I'd read a lot about the concept of reframing in my college psychology classes, and I could tell that's exactly what Dr. Stein wanted me to do in our therapy session the next day. I poured out the story of spying on Chet and his family and realizing he'd been lying to me.

I picked at a loose thread in the fabric of the office armchair and willed the scent of her lavender candle to make me feel better. It didn't work.

"At least now I know," I said, miserably. "Could I be any more of a fool and a total loser?"

"Not the words I would use to describe you. What I think is he sensed you were pulling away, wanting something more for your life than what he was offering."

"Hmmm... well, he did say he thought I was 'slipping away.' I think maybe that's why he lied about leaving his wife."

"Sounds right to me."

My eyes burned, and a couple of tears leaked out as I thought about his deception. "It hurts so bad," I said, reaching for the Kleenex she kept on the side table. I wondered if she bought boxes of tissues in bulk for all her weeping clients.

"I know. It doesn't feel good to recognize that people we've cared about aren't who we thought they were. But I want you to keep thinking about why he made this desperate move. My thought is he sensed you were getting healthier. And the healthier you got, the less you were going to want to continue a relationship on the sly that he was enjoying. My takeaway is you're changing, getting clearer about who you are and what you want and deserve for your life. And that's a good thing."

I gazed into her kind, line-filled face. "Well, when you put it that way, it sounds a lot better."

"It is better. What do you think you're going to do now?"

"I want to talk to him in person. I need that closure. And I guess that immature part of me wants to tell him what I think about the way he treated me."

"You're entitled."

"I keep beating myself up over how I could have been so gullible. And I hate myself for making such a big mistake like getting involved with a married man. Again."

"Can you see yourself having an affair with another married man in the future?"

I shivered at the thought of letting myself go down that path again. "Never. I've learned my lesson."

"Excellent. There you go. It would be nice if we could grow and mature only from our good choices, but the truth is, the most lasting life lessons turn out to come from our mistakes. And I've yet to meet anyone who hasn't made some whoppers."

I grinned. "I'm Exhibit A for whoppers alright. Speaking of which, the other thing that's eating me up is that I think it's possible we arrested the wrong guy in a murder case."

"Okay. So, what do you plan to do about that?"

"Make it right—as soon as I figure out what that is."

"Sounds good."

"Going to catch hell from the higher-ups if I've botched this thing. There goes my great reputation for closed cases."

"If that happens, you won't be the first detective, or the last, to take a fresh look at a case and change course."

I closed my eyes for a second, then opened them and gazed at my very wise therapist who had no idea what hell lay ahead for me professionally if I'd gotten the Miseau case wrong. "I would never knowingly try to put an innocent person away for a murder. Not my style. But I'm not used to striking out on the job. Maybe this is my lesson in humility. It's a bitch having to learn all these lessons at once."

She laughed, then said, "I get that. But I want you to spend time this coming week giving yourself some credit for your perseverance and courage in doing the right thing, whatever that ends up being."

I grinned back at her. "Are you sure I can't take you to my meetings with my boss and the DA if I've screwed up? I could use the backup."

"You don't need me. You're doing so much better than you give yourself credit for."

# THIRTY-FOUR

Frederick flicked on his office light and collapsed into his chair. He loosened his tie. What a day. Ten hours of presentations and meetings at the annual conference of New England arts administrators left him bone tired. All that schmoozing was exhausting.

He reached into his bottom drawer for the bottle of Chivas Regal and a glass. He poured himself a shot. He took a swig and glanced at his office phone. Thirteen messages. Oh God. He was too tired to deal with them. He'd listen tomorrow.

# THIRTY-FIVE

Wednesday morning, I stopped by Ballet Études to drop off my donation for the fund to help Mary Mikowski. I'd spoken with Mary the day before. She thanked me over and over for checking up on her. "I miss him so much," she said.

"I know you do." I promised to pay her a visit soon.

When I came into the ballet company's lobby, I was shocked to see that Dora was going with a new look. She wore a black business suit, and her hair was now one color, a pale brown, pulled back into a neat chignon.

Her attitude toward me hadn't changed, however. She smirked and said, "You again?'"

"Your lucky day. You look different."

"Yeah. Got an interview later. I figure the way things are going, it's time to look for a new job."

"Sorry to hear that. Good luck with your interview."

She shrugged and buzzed me in.

I found Frederick in his office, his head in his hands. When he looked up, I took in his red-rimmed eyes and realized he'd been crying.

"This is not a good day for me to talk, Detective."

"What's happened?"

"My...my grandfather passed away in his sleep last night. My mother found him this morning."

"I'm so sorry to hear that. Had he been ill?"

"He had a heart condition, but he was managing it well. At least I thought so. I don't understand. And now I feel so awful because he left me a voicemail yesterday when I was out of the office—said something really upsetting had happened that he wanted to talk to me about. I didn't listen to his message until this morning. Now I'll never know what was bothering him so much."

"That's all he said?"

"Yeah. Here, I'll play the message for you."

I listened and then asked, "Did your grandfather's voice always sound shaky like that?"

He rubbed his forehead. "Not this shaky. Only when he gets really upset. And I feel guilty. If I'd called him back last night, maybe I could have prevented this, you know?"

I shook my head. "There's no way you could have known. I really am sorry for your loss. Look, I won't trouble you further today. Just wanted to drop this donation off for Gus's widow." I handed him my check and was about to slip out the door when I hesitated. "One more thing. Do you know what medication your grandfather was on?"

"Same as my dad. Nitroglycerin."

———

When I got back to the office, I updated Stan on the sudden death of Gerald Gladstone, Frederick's grandfather, after leaving his grandson a message that he needed to talk to him about something upsetting "of utmost concern." I finished up with, "And guess what medication Gladstone was on?"

Stan's eyes widened. "Nitroglycerin?"

I nodded. "You up for paying a visit to Sarah Pesetsky to give her our condolences?"

"Good idea."

———

Sarah Pesetsky was wearing a black turtleneck and leggings when she opened the door thirty minutes later. Her face looked pale and pinched. "This isn't a good time, Detectives. My father passed away last night, and there are a lot of arrangements to make, as I'm sure you can understand."

"We're very sorry," I said. "We won't take up much of your time. May we come in?"

She heaved a heavy sigh. "If you must."

She opened the door wider and ushered us to seats in her living room. Once again, I was struck by the impressive artwork covering her walls—vibrant abstract paintings interspersed with her evocative photographs of the city.

"What do you want, Detectives?" she asked, as she pointedly looked at her watch.

"Your father called your son yesterday and left a voicemail he didn't listen to until this morning. Your dad said something very upsetting had happened, and he wanted to talk to Frederick as soon as possible. Do you have any idea what that was all about?"

She held her hands up and shook her head. "I haven't the foggiest. My father was eighty-six years old. Lately, I've been worried about him. He'd gotten forgetful and frankly, a little paranoid. Last week, he told me he thought someone had tried to break in while I was out at a meeting. I've been doing some reading, and unfortunately, those are two early signs of dementia."

"That's a shame," Stan said. "So, you found him this morning?"

"Yes. He likes me to wake him if he's not up by eight. When I went in, I realized he was gone."

"Would you mind if we took a look at his bedroom?" I asked.

"Lieutenant, my father had a heart condition. He died of entirely natural causes. But be my guest. The coroner's already removed his body."

"We'll just be a minute," I said.

Stan and I gloved up and headed for Gerald's last resting place. Except for the unmade bed, his bedroom appeared neat and orderly. Pictures of his late wife and children and grandchildren sat atop his dresser. His framed degrees adorned the walls, along with a plaque honoring his thirty-six years as an art history professor at Fordham University. A stack of books sat on his night table, along with a pair of reading glasses and a night light. I opened the drawer of his bedside table and found a small box of Kleenex and a bag of cough drops.

"Obviously an educated guy," Stan said. "Look at the titles of these books, all about history, art, and philosophy. Not exactly light reading."

"No kidding. Did you see that plaque? He's a retired professor."

"Makes sense."

"Let's go," I said. We took our gloves off and went back to the living room where Sarah was on her cell. I mouthed "thank you," and we let ourselves out.

On the drive back to the station, I said to Stan, "Notice anything about his bedroom?"

"Other than his being extremely well-read?"

"Stan, the guy had a heart condition. People with bad hearts keep their nitroglycerin close at hand. So why wasn't there any around on his bedside table?"

His mouth dropped open. "You're right."

I fished my phone out and dialed Chet's number. He answered on the third ring. "Hey, I need you to do an autopsy on Gerald Gladstone, Sarah Pesetksy's father. He passed away last night."

"You thinking it was suspicious?"

"Not sure, but I want to check it out."

"Okay… I really want to see you."

"Yes," I said, coldly. "I need to see you, too. I've got some things I'd like to say to you."

"You sound different. Everything okay?"

"Sure. How about I drop by your office after work—maybe around six-thirty?"

"Sounds good. Want to go for a drink?"

"Not necessary," I said, and clicked off.

Stan shot me a quizzical look. "You didn't sound overly friendly there, Cait. Anything I should know?"

"Let's just say I'm finally wising up in my old age."

"What old age?"

"I figure I'm thirty-six, going on one hundred and five."

———

Back at the office, I called Frederick Pesetsky. "Sorry to bother you again, but I wanted to ask you. Were you close to your grandfather?"

He sniffed. "Very. He was like my rock when my parents split—more of a dad to me than my dad, really."

"Uh-huh. So, have you been seeing him regularly?"

"Of course. We had a standing dinner date every Wednesday night, and we spoke often."

"Did you notice any changes in his behavior? Did he seem to you to be getting more forgetful?"

He snorted. "Lieutenant, my grandfather was sharp as a tack. He was still doing research, publishing articles in art history journals. There was nothing wrong with his brain power."

"Did he ever seem paranoid to you? Telling you that he

was worried someone might be breaking into your mom's condo?"

"No! Of course not. My grandfather was the sanest person I know. Where are you getting this?"

I didn't answer. "One last question. Do you happen to know the name of your grandfather's physician?"

"Hughes. Dr. Melvin Hughes. He's a nice guy. I used to take my grandfather to his appointments if Mom was busy. He was very fond of my grandfather. Why do you ask?"

Again, I didn't answer. All I said was, "I really appreciate your help" and repeated my condolences before ending the call.

I turned to Stan. "Frederick denies that his grandfather was either forgetful or paranoid. Says he saw him every week, and his mental faculties were fine. The guy was still writing and publishing."

Stan pursed his lips. "You thinking what I'm thinking?"

"Unfortunately."

———

I got to Chet's office right on time. This was it. My heart thumped in my chest as I walked into his office.

He jumped up, shut the door and attempted to pull me into his arms.

I pushed him away. "I wanted to tell you two things, Chet. First, we are over. Fini. And second, congratulations on your wife's pregnancy. I'm delighted for you both."

His face blanched. "How... how did you know?"

"Decided to do a little reconnaissance last weekend. How was your picnic, by the way?"

"Look... Cait, I can explain"—

"No, I don't think you can. You're a liar and a cheat, and I was stupid enough to fall for you. I pity your next victim, and

I'm very sorry for your wife. She was the one making those threatening phone calls to me, wasn't she?"

He hung his head. "I found something in our basement, one of those gadgets that distorts your voice. I was pretty shook up when I found it. It just seems so... out of character for my wife."

"Apparently not. The two of you deserve one another."

"You're not going to press charges against her, are you? I'm thinking about my kids—and both our careers if this comes out."

"I have no idea. Probably not if she stops. But if you want to keep your family together, you both need help, professional help."

He ran his hands through his hair, then wiped a sheen of perspiration off his brow. "You're right. I'm really sorry."

"Why did you lie to me? Make up that cock and bull story about how you and Marian were going to separate?"

He licked his lips. "I suppose I was buying time. I couldn't bear to lose you."

"Well, Chet, that ship has sailed."

"I'll always love you, you know," he said, his voice cracking.

"No, I don't think so. Love is about trust and honesty. And respect for the other person."

"You can cut the 'holier than thou' crap, Cait. This all began when you came on to me. And you certainly knew I was married."

A wave of heat crossed my face. "I don't recall your turning me down, but you're right. I made a lousy decision to get involved with you. But there's a basic difference between you and me."

"What?"

"I never lied to you."

"I know. But can we at least be friends?" He sounded like a whiny kid begging for a reprieve from a timeout.

"I'm not your friend, Chet. But I value your professional skills, and I will certainly be civil."

"So that's it then? You're just going to throw away everything we've had together?"

"That's the plan. And if I hear one more word from your wife, she's going down."

# THIRTY-SIX

I couldn't decide whether I was more relieved or heartbroken after breaking things off with Chet for good. Maybe both? But on the drive home that night in a spring rainstorm, the need to sort out my feelings took a backseat to the need to focus on the road.

I made a mental note to invest in a pair of new windshield wipers. The rain poured down in buckets and my tired wipers couldn't keep up. I probably should have pulled over and waited the storm out, but I was so eager to retreat to my cocoon of an apartment. By the time I got home, I was sweating from the effort to drive through the storm.

Once inside, I stripped off and took a long, hot shower. As I poured a generous helping of shampoo into my fingers and worked it into my scalp, the song "Gonna Wash That Man Right Out of My Hair" from the old musical *South Pacific* floated into my brain. I scrubbed harder.

Later that night, I sat in the dark, the only light coming from my Sandalwood candle and the streetlights outside. I sipped a glass of white wine and realized I felt lighter. I knew I'd be grieving for Chet, or maybe my fantasy of him, for a while, but it felt good to have finally said to him, as well as myself, 'Enough.'

Hank called around nine. "You feeling better?" he asked in that deep voice I found so appealing.

"I really am," I said. "I'm so sorry I had to cancel on you."

"Understood. Listen, Jack's not with me this week. How do you feel about trying again to have dinner Friday night?"

"Love to. And tell me how your week with Jack was."

"Great." He went on to describe their latest Lego project, an enormous castle they'd attached to the space station they'd built earlier. "What can I say? He's into fairy tales featuring humongous castles, and he says he wants to be an astronaut and explore Mars someday, so why not put them together?"

I laughed. "Works for me. You're a good dad." A sliver of pain sliced through me. I'd idolized my father and the work he did, but he'd always been too busy to spend much time with me.

We chatted for a few more minutes and as we were about to end the conversation, Hank said, "You sound different."

"Really?"

"Yeah. Anything you care to share?"

"Working through some things. Maybe talk more in person Friday night?"

"Can't wait."

———

The next morning, I wrote up a request to subpoena Gus's phone records. By that afternoon, my request had been approved. Stan and I pored over the records and cross-checked numbers. Mostly routine stuff—calls to Mary's doctors, their insurance company, and the pharmacy where Gus filled his wife's prescriptions. But my eyes widened when we discovered that in the days before his murder, Gus had called Sarah Pesetsky. Twice. He'd made the last call the night before he died.

"Time to subpoena her bank records?" Stan asked.

"Yup."

By Friday afternoon, we'd gotten hold of Sarah Pesetsky's bank records. Sure enough, she'd withdrawn $5,000 in cash from her bank account ten days before Gus had been shot.

"We can't know for sure that Gus was blackmailing her," Stan said. "Maybe she was loaning him the money for his wife's treatment."

"In cash? Why not a check?"

"True."

"Let's pay Victor's ex another visit. See what she says."

————

Sarah Pesetsky's lips pressed into a thin straight line when she opened the door to us. Today she wore a long tunic with geometric shapes and black leggings and boots. Her heavy makeup couldn't quite conceal the dark circles beneath her eyes. "You two again? This is starting to feel like harassment. I'm just getting ready to go out."

"This won't take long," I assured her. "We have a few more questions for you."

"Oh, all right. Come in."

We settled in the living room. Stan and I sat on her black leather couch, while she took a seat in the beige armchair across from us.

"What do you need to know?" she asked.

"Can you explain the two phone calls Gus Mikowski made to you and your withdrawal of $5,000 in cash from your bank account?"

Her shoulders stiffened. "Checking up on me, huh? Well, that's easily explained. Surely, you've heard his wife Mary is very ill. He phoned me and asked me for a loan. Which I gave him."

"Was there a reason you withdrew the money in cash?" Stan asked.

She shrugged. "He asked for cash. I have no idea why, but he was so distraught about his wife I didn't press him about it."

"The second phone call to you took place the night before he was shot. Was he asking for another loan?" I asked.

She fingered a stray lock of hair that had escaped from her chignon, and I noticed the slight tremor in her hand. "No, not at all. Actually, he was calling to thank me again for the loan. Said it made a huge difference. Mary would be able to start a course of some new treatment."

"Do you own a gun, Ms. Pesetsky?" I asked.

She snorted. "What is this? You think I murdered poor Gus?"

"Just routinely investigating. Do you?"

"My father had one, I think. But he mentioned a few months ago that it was missing. He thought maybe our cleaning lady had swiped it. At the time, I thought that was more of his paranoia. But when I checked his room and the study, I couldn't find it anywhere."

"Do you recall if his gun was a 38?" I asked.

She shrugged. "Absolutely no idea. I never used it." She stood up. "If there's nothing else, I need to go. I have an appointment to discuss my father's memorial service."

Stan and I rose as well. "Of course," I said, smoothly. "We'll be in touch."

She pursed her lips. "I hope there'll be no need to. This has been a very difficult time, and frankly, I don't need any more aggravation."

I nodded at her as she held the door for us. "Neither do we," I said.

On the drive back to the station, I asked Stan to put in a call to check on whether any guns were registered to Sarah Peset-sky's father, Gerald Gladstone. Or to Sarah Pesetsky.

"Right on it."

The call back came in as we were gathering our stuff and getting ready to call it a day.

"Uh-huh," Stan said. "Thanks for your help."

My pulse quickened. "What gives?"

"Sarah Pesetsky was telling the truth. A gun was registered to her father."

"What caliber?"

"38."

"Holy shit. Did he ever report it stolen?"

"That would be no," Stan said.

# THIRTY-SEVEN

Friday night, I spent extra time on my makeup. I even put on some purple eyes shadow to match my dress. Even though Hank and I had been out before, in some ways, this felt like a first date—at least the first date since Chet and I were officially over. I knew I didn't want to rush into anything with Hank, but I was eager to spend the evening with a really nice guy who didn't appear to harbor any deep dark secrets—like a pregnant wife he had no intention of leaving.

Hank arrived right on time, a wide grin on his face and his black curly hair looking damp from what I assumed must have been a recent shower. "You look fantastic. I don't think I've ever seen you in a dress. That color looks amazing on you."

I gave him a tremulous grin. I realized I was nervous, as though this were some sort of coming out event. Which, in a way, it was. "Thanks. Periwinkle's one of my favorites. And I never get to wear dresses on duty. Besides, I felt like celebrating spring."

"Well, you're going to fit right in at Mezcal. Every time I

pass the building with those brightly colored mural walls, I think about going there. But I never have. How about you?"

"I've been there, but not in a long time." This was one of the downsides about having a relationship with a married man. You never went anywhere where you might be spotted.

Twenty minutes later, we were seated at a cozy corner table sipping our drinks, a Mexican beer for Hank and a margarita for me. We chatted about his week, and then he asked me how my work was going.

"Don't ask," I told him. "Do I look like I have mud on my face?"

He peered at me closely and then took off his glasses and leaned closer.

I inhaled the scent of his musky cologne, and a sliver of excitement wove through my body.

"Nope. Not yet. No sign of mud."

"Stay tuned."

The waiter brought out warm chips and salsa, and we dove in. After my fourth grab of chips, I pushed the basket toward Hank. "I'll never be able to eat dinner if I keep munching on these."

We decided on the *enchiladas de mole* and after giving our order to the waiter, Hank leaned back in his seat and said, "So, you mentioned working through some things. You feel like sharing?"

I took a deep breath. "I finally ended my—involvement. It wasn't a healthy relationship for me, or for him. I know I made the right decision, but—"

"But it's still hard, isn't it?"

"Yeah. I mean, I feel relieved, but also sad, and really anxious—like I've jumped off a cliff and I'm praying for a soft landing."

"I've been there. Endings are rough. When my wife left me, it was like my whole world felt off-kilter and I was stumbling around in the fog trying to find my footing. All I can say is it does get better."

I struggled to smile. "I'm counting on it."

"And you know I'm dying to ask you what happened, and I'm not going to."

"Kind of like I'm dying to ask you about your marriage, but I won't tread there."

He grinned. "Exactly. But I am curious about one thing. Did this guy sour you on relationships?"

I hesitated, wondering if I was ready to be open with Hank about my lousy romantic choices. Hell, might as well find out if he could handle who I really was—or maybe had been. I set my drink down and said, "No. But I don't want a repeat of my past. I've had this habit of getting involved with married guys. My relationships all end badly, and I'm working on having a better relationship with myself, if that makes any sense."

He reached for my hand. "Change is tough. And you're smart to focus on getting right with yourself."

"You're making me feel better already."

He leaned forward and gazed at me intently. "I'm glad. But just so you know, I'm not married. If all you want from me is friendship, you have it. And if you ever want more, like that old song says, 'I'll Be Around.'"

My heart hammered in my chest, and I squeezed his hand. "Thank you for that. I like you, Hank, but I'm scared. If we can take things really, really, slowly—like snail slowly, I think I'm ready for 'more.'"

A huge smile spread across his face, and the laugh lines around his dark brown eyes crinkled. He picked up his beer and motioned for me to pick up my margarita. I complied, and we clinked glasses. "To the future," he said.

———

After dinner, we took a long walk around the harbor. For the first time, Hank held my hand. I let myself enjoy the warmth of his hand, and as I inhaled the sea scent, a sense of peace fell over me.

And when he brought me home, he stroked my cheek and leaned down and kissed me gently for the first time. He tasted so good, felt so good. I wrapped my arms around him and pulled him in closer.

But to my surprise, he abruptly ended the kiss.

Breathing hard, he said, "I could kiss you forever, Caitlin, but damned if I'm going to move too fast and mess this up." Then he turned and strode away, leaving me standing in the doorway.

I already missed the warmth of his arms, but I was so touched that he was determined to do what I'd asked him to— go slowly.

When I closed my door, I moved to my old CD collection and searched for my favorite Frank Sinatra album, *In the Wee Small Hours.* As I got ready for bed, I listened to his poignant interpretation of "I'll Be Around." And then I fell asleep thinking about the look on Hank's face when I told him I was ready for 'more.'

———

Saturday morning, I went for an early run, showered, and fixed myself an English muffin lathered in creamy peanut butter. As I inhaled two cups of coffee, I thought about Hank and wondered when I might hear from him again. I felt like a teenager in the throes of a new crush. How could I already be so smitten when I'd so recently broken off things with Chet? Was I that fickle? Or had my relationship with Chet been dying for a long time?

No idea, but I had to turn my attention to the case. I decided to pay a visit to Mary to see how she was doing. And what she thought of the likelihood Gus had asked Sarah Pesetsky for a loan.

---

When Mary opened the door wearing a faded housecoat, she looked even tinier and frailer than I remembered. But her smile was warm as she ushered me inside and offered me some tea. "I just made some."

"I'm good. Thanks."

We settled on her threadbare rose-colored couch. She pulled a flowery sky-blue afghan over her knees. "Don't know why I'm always so cold."

"That's a beautiful afghan. Did you make it?"

"I did. After I couldn't work anymore, it was a way to pass the time."

The thought of this sweet lady sitting here day after day by herself while Gus was at work made me so sad. And now he was never coming home. This was the part of being a homicide detective I hated the most—witnessing the suffering of the folks left behind. "How are you holding up?" I asked.

"Oh well, you know, it's like half of me is gone. We were so close. And the thought of somebody shooting him…" Her eyes grew watery. "Is there any news, Lieutenant?"

"Nothing definite. But I do have a question for you about the $5,000 you found in your account. Do you think there's any possibility that Sarah Pesetsky might have loaned Gus the money?"

"Victor's ex? I can't imagine that. To tell you the truth, Gus thought she was—well, snooty—treated him like he was beneath her. Nothing like Lydia, who was always so kind and took time to talk with him. He was very fond of that one."

"So, you don't think there's a possibility Gus approached Sarah about a loan?"

She shook her head. "No. My Gus had his pride. I could

see him maybe asking Victor or Frederick for a loan, but not her."

"That's helpful, Mary. By the way, has Frederick contacted you?"

Her face brightened. "He has. He's been collecting donations for my treatment. I'm so grateful."

"Are you going ahead then with the treatment?"

"I am. I thought about it. Gus would have wanted me to."

"I know he would have. And has Beth been around at all?"

"Oh yes, she's been a lifesaver. Checks on me every day."

"Good. She seems very nice."

"She is. You'll let me know if you figure out who killed my Gus?"

"Absolutely."

———

When I got back to my car, I checked my phone and found a text from Hank. "Had a wonderful time last night. Are you still okay with 'more'?"

I sent him a smiley face back. Corny, but what the heck?

Three minutes later, I got another text from him. "Is it moving too fast to see you tomorrow afternoon? Maybe take a road trip to Mystic to the aquarium?"

I smiled. Hank really was a science geek. I loved it. And I loved the normalcy of this—going places, public places, with a guy who was definitely growing on me.

I texted him back: "You're on. Want to come over beforehand for brunch around eleven?"

"Sounds great."

When I got back to my apartment, I launched into a cleaning frenzy. I realized I wanted my place to look inviting—well, at least clean.

After that, I did laundry and went shopping for my brunch with Hank. Mom called around four. I felt a stab of guilt for not being a better daughter. I'd been so wrapped up in the case and my personal life I hadn't called her all week.

"I'm so sorry I haven't been in better touch," I told her.

"Oh honey, I know you're busy. Everything going okay?"

"It is. You want to grab some dinner together tonight?"

She hesitated, then said, "Wish I could, but I have other plans."

"Plans?" I knew my mom didn't like to drive at night.

"Well, believe it or not, I've met someone. He's taking me to dinner." Her voice sounded higher, lighter, than usual.

My stomach lurched. I wanted my mother to be happy, but somehow, I'd never pictured her with anyone but my dad. "Wow! That's great. Who's the lucky guy?"

"Actually, he's an admissions counselor for Yale's non-degree program. I've been thinking about going back to school and thought I'd try taking some pre-requisites for the grad program in sociology."

"That's super, Mom. You always wanted to go to grad school."

"It's a little scary. I mean it's been ages since I was in a classroom."

"You'll do fine. You loved school. Dad always said he wouldn't have gotten through his sociology classes without your help."

"He did, didn't he?" I could hear the smile in her voice.

"So, how did this hot date come about?"

She giggled. "Not sure it qualifies as 'hot,' but when I went for my admissions appointment, I think he could tell I was really nervous. He said the professors are always telling him they love their non-traditional students, because we're so focused and appreciative. Then he told me about switching his career to higher ed after being in pharmaceutical sales, and how anxious he'd been when he started over in his forties."

"He sounds really nice, Mom. And I'm so happy you're doing something for yourself that you've always wanted to."

"Thanks, honey. So, anything new with you?"

I swallowed. Where to begin? "Do you want the good news or the bad news?"

"Hmmm... hit me with the bad news first."

"Bad news is I may have pooched an investigation and arrested the wrong person."

"Oh dear. I'm so sorry. But I know you'll make it right."

"Hope so, but the fallout with my captain's not going to be pretty. I'm actually glad Dad isn't around to see me make a big, fat mess." I put my hand over my mouth. Had I really just told my mom I was glad my dad was dead?

She didn't seem to mind. "Now Caitlin, contrary to the impression he may have given you, your father had more than one investigation in his career where he had to do some major backpedaling. It happens."

My mouth gaped open. "Really?"

"Really. Nobody gets it right all the time."

"Dad always seemed so... in control, always on top of things."

"I think he wanted you kids to see him that way, even after you were adults. Sometimes he'd be in a terrible mood, fretting over some case, and the minute you kids came over, he'd act like everything was hunky-dory. But believe me, he had his mishaps. Now tell me, what's your good news?"

"Well, I finally ended things with Chet. And I've had a couple of dates with a guy who teaches at Melissa's middle school."

"Is he married?"

"Divorced, and he has a little boy who lives with him half-time. He's so nice, Mom. We've agreed to take things slowly, but I like him."

"Well, hallelujah! I'm so glad you got rid of Chet. I've been worried about you. And it must feel good to go out with someone who's actually available. What's his name?"

"Hank. I think you'd like him, Mom. He teaches science, loves kids."

"Sounds great. When do I get to meet him?'

I laughed. "Not so fast! We're barely dating. But if it turns into anything, of course, I want you to meet him."

"I'm counting on it."

"So, what's the name of this guy you're going out with tonight?"

"Peter Madonia."

"Where's he taking you?"

"Union League Café."

"He likes you, Mom. Most romantic French restaurant in the city."

"Do you realize how long it's been since I've had a date with anyone other than your father?"

"My therapist told me about this book that says you have to 'feel the fear and do it anyway.'"

"Good advice. So, you up for lunch tomorrow?"

"Sorry, but Hank's coming over for brunch, and then we're going to the aquarium. How about lunch next Saturday? I want the lowdown on your date."

"And I want the lowdown on yours."

"Deal," I said.

After we hung up, I sat on the couch for a long time staring out the window as a light drizzle fell. I opened my window a crack to enjoy the scent of the wet rain. I thought about all the changes going on in my mom's life, and my own. I couldn't decide which felt weirder—me dating someone who wasn't married, or Mom going out with a new man and returning to school. A definite toss-up.

My reverie was interrupted by a knock at my door. When I peeked through the peep hole, my stomach lurched. Chet's wife Marian stood there. What in the world?

Cautiously, I opened the door. She wore a robin's blue rain-coat that complemented her baby blue eyes. With her petite baby bump, she looked like an ad for a maternity catalogue: "You too can look this adorable while pregnant."

"May I come in?" She pushed her way past me before I could respond.

She turned around to face me. "I need to know if it's really over, this thing between you and my husband."

"Yes, and I bet you're pretty sure about that since you haven't made any of those middle-of-the-night phone calls lately. Did you really think that was a good idea to threaten a police officer? I could have arrested you."

"Don't think so. Then you would have had to admit what you were doing. I doubt your boss would have approved your carrying on an adulterous affair with the medical examiner."

The heat of my own guilt and embarrassment swept through my body. "Look, it's over. I'm sorry."

Spittle formed around the edges of her mouth. "You're sorry? Oh, that's rich. You think fucking someone else's husband, a guy with two children who need him and another one on the way, is okay? You can make it all better by saying, 'Oops! My bad.' Well, it's not that easy."

"I get that. I'm not sure what you're doing here if you don't want my apology."

"I want you to know what total scum you are. I hope you burn in hell. And in case you think you're anything special, you're not the first. I've been dealing with Chet's roving eye for years."

*Why didn't that surprise me?* "Okay. Anything else you'd like to say to me before I ask you to leave?"

"You probably thought my husband loved you, cared about you. Well, you were just another disgusting piece of tail. He finally admitted he's got a sex addiction. He's going for treatment. What's your excuse for what you did?"

Tears gathered behind my eyelids. "I have none. I've made some very poor choices in my personal life. Getting involved with your husband was one of them. But I too have sought treatment. And you'll never again have to worry about me invading your life. Or your husband's."

"Let's hope so," she said and strode past me.

"I really am sorry."

"Save it." She slammed the door on her way out.

I sank down on the couch and buried my face in my hands. My whole body shook. I knew I deserved every bit of her scorn and fury. But it still hurt—especially because she was right. Chet was scum and claiming he had a sex addiction sounded like a great excuse for being a serial cheater, but I wasn't much better.

What a rotten thing I'd done to get involved with him and not even think about what I was doing to his wife, his kids. No wonder she didn't want an apology from me. She only wanted to let me know just what a piece of shit I was. And could I really blame her? How understanding and forgiving would I have been in her shoes?

Dr. Stein always reminded me to stop beating myself up over whatever choices I'd made in the past. But forgiving myself was so hard.

At least I felt "cured." Getting involved with another married man held zilch appeal.

An image of Hank floated across my mind. He was so damned healthy. And kind. Hanging out with him felt like slipping into a different universe—where people were honest and caring. And good. I wanted all of that in my life.

# THIRTY-EIGHT

"These eggs are amazing," Hank said, as he patted his stomach and then grabbed a second helping from the serving dish I'd kept on a warming tray.

I grinned at him. "I make them in a double-boiler, a trick my mom taught me."

"She must be a good teacher. What's your mom like?"

"She's really nice, warm, always there for my brothers and me. And she's super smart. Going back to school and starting to date again."

"She sounds a lot like you."

Heat flooded my face. "I wish."

"Oh, come on."

"I always felt gangly and awkward around her. She's really pretty and petite. I'm built like my dad—sturdy and tall."

"Speaking personally, 'sturdy and tall' sounds mighty appealing." His eyes twinkled.

"Hank Miller, are you flirting with me?"

"How did you guess?" He reached across the table for my hand.

———

I loved the museum, especially the shark exhibit. Hank couldn't resist going into teacher mode, pointing out the bull, sand-bar, and sand-tiger sharks and discussing their differences. His excitement was contagious, even though I teased him about his "mini-lectures." I couldn't help thinking it would have been nice to have such an enthusiastic science teacher in junior high. Mr. Mottolese, my eighth-grade science teacher, was limping toward retirement. Mostly, he yelled at us to keep quiet and fill out boring work sheets.

"Is this another place you take your students?" I asked.

"I do. And Jack, too." He pulled out his phone and scrolled through his pictures. "This is Jack at the Touch Habitat. He loves getting to touch the baby sharks."

I studied the picture and wondered if I'd ever get to meet this adorable little guy with the curly dark hair and gap-toothed grin. "He looks like you. I take it the Tooth Fairy has been to your house."

"Oh yeah. The Tooth Fairy always makes it to both houses. Jack really cleans up."

"The advantage of having divorced parents, I guess."

Hank's face clouded over. "Jack would much rather have parents who were together. But I wasn't able to give him that."

I reached for his hand and squeezed it. "Maybe not, but he has you for a dad. That makes him lucky."

———

My good mood from spending time with Hank over the weekend dissipated pretty quickly Monday morning when I took one look at Stan's drawn face and the bags beneath his eyes.

"You look like hell. What's going on?"

"Joey came up to visit this weekend and insisted on taking me out to dinner to celebrate my recovery. We went to Zinc's and—"

"Nice place," I said.

"Very. So, who do you think we ran into?"

"Oh, no."

"Oh yes. JoAnne and her fat cat fiancé were all over each other, and she was wearing a rock the size of Gibraltar."

"No fun at all. I'm so sorry."

He rubbed his temple. "The thing is, I think I'm doing better and then seeing her with my replacement... it was awful. All I wanted to do was drink my way back into oblivion."

"You didn't, did you?"

"No. Joey made me call my sponsor who helped me make it through the weekend. No sleep, but I'm here."

"I'm glad. You've got people who are really in your corner, Stan—including me."

"I know. I just have to get through this—and stay away from fancy restaurants where my ex might be. She's finally living the high life she always wanted."

"I hear it's over-rated."

"I wish. You look great, by the way. Good weekend?'

"Yup."

"Did you spend time with you know who?"

"Believe it or not, old married Chet is officially history."

"No kidding. Does this mean we're both in recovery?"

I snorted. "You got it."

"So, what made you cut the strings?"

"A bunch of stuff—getting into therapy, realizing he was playing me, finally figuring out this was just messed up... not fair to his family and definitely unhealthy for me."

He held up his hand, and we high-fived. "I'm happy for you, Cait. So, anything new on the case?"

I filled him in on my visit to Mary. "She doesn't think there's any way Gus would have asked Sarah Pesetsky for a loan. Ten to one he was shaking her down."

"What next?"

Before I could answer, our office phone rang. I picked up and Chet, sounding formal and distant, told me he was calling to report the results of the autopsy on Gerald Gladstone. "No obvious signs of foul play," he reported. "Looks like a heart attack. The odd thing is his heart didn't look that bad. He must have been on nitroglycerin. It should have controlled things."

*Unless he reached for it, and it wasn't there.* "Thanks, Chet. Believe it or not, this is helpful."

"You doing okay?" he said, his voice markedly softer.

"Good."

"I miss you, Cait."

Amazingly, I didn't feel the usual pull back into his web. "Gotta go," I said. "Thanks again."

I clicked off, took a deep breath, and talked to Stan about Chet's report. "No way to prove it, but what do you want to bet Sarah Pesetsky removed her father's nitroglycerin from his bedside table?"

Stan's eyes widened. "Why would she do that?"

"Maybe he'd discovered something she didn't want him to talk to his grandson about."

"Holy shit."

"I'm going to put in a call to Gerald Gladstone's doctor— find out his take on his patient's death."

"Good idea. He probably won't talk to you, though. Patient privacy and all that."

"You never know and even if we can't build a case against her for killing him, it'll come in handy when we question her."

———

I finally got hold of Dr. Hughes after lunch and explained I had a few questions about his former patient in connection with a homicide investigation.

"Surely you don't think Gerald was murdered," he said.

"Not necessarily. He may have had information pertinent

to another homicide. Can you tell me about his medical condition prior to his death?"

"Lieutenant, I'm not free to discuss my patients' conditions or treatment with you. It's a matter of privacy."

"I understand, but Gerald Gladstone is dead. He's no longer your patient, and as I said, this is a homicide investigation."

He sighed. "All right. But I know very little, and I must ask you to keep this confidential and keep my name out of your investigation. Gerald had a mild heart condition for which I prescribed nitroglycerin. He appeared to me to be managing his condition well."

"Did you observe any cognitive deterioration? Signs of confusion or memory loss?"

"Absolutely not. He knew I was interested in art and always had recommendations for books I might like, and upcoming exhibits I might want to see. He was very sharp."

"Interesting. Was there anything unusual or strange that you noticed or observed in treating him recently?"

Dr. Hughes seemed to hesitate for a moment. Finally, he said, "His daughter telephoned me last week, wanting a refill of his nitroglycerin. Claimed he was getting forgetful and had misplaced his medication. I thought it was odd because I hadn't noticed any cognitive decline in her father. But I did re-up his meds."

"Dr. Hughes, were you surprised when you learned that he'd died of a heart attack?"

Another pause. "It seemed to me he was doing well, but I suppose one never knows. I have a patient waiting, so if there's nothing else…"

"Of course." I thanked him for his help and after hanging up, I turned to Stan and told him about Sarah wanting a refill of her father's medication, claiming he'd lost it. "And Dr. Hughes had the same assessment Frederick Pesetsky had about his grandfather. No sign of cognitive decline whatsoever."

Stan heaved a sigh. "You thinking what I'm thinking?"

"Yup. You ready for having Captain rip a hole—make that two holes—you know where?"

"Not really, but I don't think we've got a choice at this point."

# THIRTY-NINE

Captain Singleton ushered us into his office, took one look at our faces, and said, "Why do I think this is bad news?"

"Sir, I really apologize, but we think it's possible that we arrested the wrong person for Lydia Miseau's death," I said.

"What? Please tell me you're kidding. You told me you had everything you needed: means, motive, opportunity. What the hell is going on?" His dark eyes glittered, and I was surprised sparks weren't coming out of his shaved head.

"The fatal shooting of the company's custodian led us to dig further. We think the murders may be connected, and that Gus was blackmailing Sarah Pesetsky, Victor Pesetsky's ex-wife."

I proceeded to lay it all out—the phone calls Gus had made to Sarah, the $5,000 deposited into his account, matching the amount Sarah had withdrawn in cash from her bank, and Sarah's access to nitroglycerin due to her late father's heart condition. "Sarah was working on a photography project and spending lots of time in the dressing rooms. Gus may have witnessed her tampering with Miseau's makeup and decided to blackmail her to get money for his wife's cancer treatments."

"Why didn't you check her out before you arrested Victor Pesetsky?"

"We interviewed her. But Victor just seemed so obvious, what with his wife's cheating and the insurance settlement."

Captain shook his head and scowled at us. "You should know by now to thoroughly investigate every possibility. Ex-spouses are obvious people to check out, especially if they've had easy access to the crime scene. I don't believe this!"

I hung my head, careful not to remind him that both he and the DA had signed off on our making an arrest. "All I can say is we honestly thought we had the right guy. But there's more."

"What?"

Stan broke in then. "Gus was shot with a 38. A Smith and Wesson 38 was registered to Sarah's father, Gerald Gladstone. Sarah Pesetsky claims the gun was stolen. She also said she loaned money to Gus because he asked her for a loan, in cash, by the way. But Mary, Gus's widow, said her husband disliked Sarah and would never have approached her to borrow money."

Captain cracked his knuckles several times, his go-to move when he was really upset.

"What else?" he asked, giving me his best death stare.

"Sarah claimed her father was growing forgetful. She called his doctor and asked for a refill of his nitroglycerin. Said he'd misplaced his meds. But both Gerald's grandson, Frederick Pesetsky, and his physician insist he was totally with it mentally. And the night he died, he called Frederick and said he had something very upsetting to discuss with him. He didn't live long enough to tell him what it was."

Captain's mouth gaped open. "Are you saying Sarah Pesetsky may also have killed her own father?"

I shrugged. "We don't have enough evidence to prove that. But when Stan and I looked at his bedroom, the day after he died, there was no nitroglycerin on his bedside table. And Chet says his heart didn't look that bad, and his meds should have controlled any problems. There's no way to prove she took his meds away, but it doesn't make sense he wouldn't keep his pills close by."

Captain bit his lip and glared first at me, then at Stan. "I'm disappointed in both of you. You're supposed to be my best detectives, and instead, your shoddy investigation makes us all look bad."

"I really am sorry," I said. "We honestly thought we got it right."

"Yeah, yeah. All right, nothing to do but push ahead. Question the Pesetsky woman again."

"Will do. And I want to get a search warrant for her home. We want to see if she has a pill grinder or a 38."

He nodded. "Okay. Now get out of here and get to work. Trust me, it's going to take a while for you two to get off my shit list."

"Understood," I said, as Stan and I stood and slunk out the door.

Stan squeezed my arm as soon as we closed Captain's door. "The good news is he didn't put us back on parking meter patrol."

"Not yet. No guarantees we won't end up there."

————

Stan insisted we needed decent coffee to recover from our meeting with Captain. He made a Starbucks run while I wrote up the request for a search warrant.

When he got back, he said, "You want to pay a visit to Sarah now, or wait until tomorrow?"

"No time like the present. Let's roll."

———

Someone we'd never seen before, a silver-haired woman with a weathered face wearing jeans and a faded Red Sox sweat-shirt, answered the door at Pesetsky's condo. "May I help you?" she asked.

We held up our badges. "Lieutenant O'Connor and Sergeant Bisso. Is Ms. Pesetsky available?"

"Let me check. She goes in and out a lot."

"And you are?" I asked.

"Jackie Kish. I'm with Lucianus Home Services. I'm helping Ms. Pesetsky clear out her father's possessions. I'll see if she's in her studio."

She headed down the hall, which was now lined with boxes of old books and men's clothing. Apparently, Sarah was wasting no time getting rid of her father's possessions.

"You again?" she said, as she strode down the hall with Jackie trailing behind. "What can you possibly want now?"

"Can we sit down? We have a few more questions for you."

"Fine," she said, her frosty tone making it clear it wasn't fine at all. She gestured for us to follow her into the living room. "Jackie, can you finish packing up Dr. Gladstone's suits?"

"Of course," she said, disappearing down the hall.

Sarah turned back to us. "What is it now?"

"The gun registered to your father was a 38. The same caliber that killed Gus Mikowski," I said.

She held her hands up. "So? Do you know how many thousands of 38 caliber guns there are in this area? If you're implying that I shot Gus, you'll have to do better than that! I told you—I loaned him money because his wife was ill. End of story." Her ice blue eyes glared at me, as though daring me to question her word.

"Was Gus Mikowski blackmailing you because he'd seen you tamper with Lydia's makeup the day of her death?" Stan asked.

"Don't be ridiculous! You arrested Victor for killing his little trophy wife, didn't you? I had nothing to do with it. Is this the thanks I get for doing a good deed—helping Gus out? The poor man was terrified to lose his wife."

"That's true," I said. "But most people asking for a $5,000 loan don't ask for it in cash."

"I told you. I have no idea why he wanted the money in cash. He was distraught. I was trying to help him."

"Okay. Was your father on nitroglycerin?" I asked, changing the subject.

"Yes, like millions of other people who have heart conditions. But if you're implying I used his nitroglycerin to harm Lydia, that's absurd. You arrested Victor, who had, as I understand, plenty of reasons to get rid of his child bride. She was only twenty-three when he left his family for her."

"And how did you feel about Lydia Miseau?"

She shrugged. "Brilliant dancer. Not my favorite person, but she was Victor's problem, not mine."

We were getting nowhere fast. The woman had an answer for everything. "One other thing," I said. "You told us your father was getting forgetful, a little paranoid. Your son Frederick denies his grandfather was showing any signs of cognitive decline."

"Dad was very good at hiding his issues, putting on a game face, especially with Frederick, whom he adored. But I lived with my father and had a front row seat to his deterioration. It was heart-breaking, actually. My dad had been a brilliant man."

"Yes. One thing that puzzled me was why we saw no nitroglycerin on his bedside table when we looked into his bedroom," I said. "It would seem as though you would have been careful that your father had easy access to his medication."

She blinked several times, and her eyebrows knitted together.

Aha, I thought. For once, she was struggling to come up with a logical explanation.

Finally, she said, "I thought I had checked that night before I went to bed. But Dad had been doing strange things with his meds. I suppose he could have put them away somewhere. I guess we'll never know."

"We'll never know" may have been the most truthful statement she'd made to us. Also, the most frustrating.

"If we have more questions, we'll be in touch," I said, as Stan and I stood up.

"I really hope not." She strode to the front door and opened it for us. "I resent these questions and your implications when all I did was try to help Gus and take care of my elderly father. I advise you to be very careful about harassing innocent people and making false accusations, or you may be facing a lawsuit—not to mention the loss of your badges."

Neither one of us responded to her threat. She slammed the door behind us, and I turned to Stan. "One more shit list we've landed on. And all we've got is a boatload of suspicions and no proof."

"Hey, we can't win 'em all."

I knew he was trying to cheer me up, but the thought that Sarah Pesetsky might well have murdered two, maybe even three, people and had a good chance of getting away with her crimes made me nauseous.

———

At home that night, all I could stomach was ginger ale and saltine crackers. Melissa called around eight, sounding all bubbly and excited. "I ran into Hank at school today. The guy was glowing—said you had two dates this past weekend."

"We did. We had a great time," I said, trying to sound more cheerful than I felt.

"What's wrong? Please don't tell me you're going to hurt Hank. He's falling hard for you."

"No, no. That's not it. We really did have a wonderful time. Hank's great."

"So why do you sound so flat?"

"It's a case I'm working on. It's got me down—can't really talk about it."

"Okay. And what about Chet? Is he still in the picture?"

"Nope."

"Yes!" she shouted. "I was wondering when you'd come to your senses. He was no good for you, Cait."

I picked at a loose thread on my afghan, which made me think about poor Mary Miskowski. I pulled my concentration back to talking to Melissa. "Yeah. So, I'm figuring out. But in a way, I'm grieving. It's a loss of a relationship that meant a lot to me, even if it was wrong."

"I get that, Cait. I do. But you deserve so much better. And suppose Chet really had left his wife for you? I know you would have beaten yourself up over destroying a family, hurting his kids."

"You're right. It was stupid and wrong. I was playing with fire, and I'm the one who got burned. But honestly? I think I'm cured. The thought of getting involved with another married man makes me want to puke."

Melissa snorted. "Well, good, because I happen to know a very unmarried man who really likes you."

"I like him, too. But I don't want him to be just a rebound person in my life. I need to take things really slowly."

"If I know Hank, he'll be fine with that. His eyes light up when he talks about you. This is the first time since his divorce that I've seen him interested in dating anyone."

"Good to know. You're cheering me up."

And she was. We chatted for a few more minutes and I promised to join her family Friday night for pizza. I adored her kids, and Hank had his son with him this weekend. I couldn't help wondering if and when I'd ever get to meet Jack.

# FORTY

By the next morning, Stan and I had our search warrant and headed to Sarah Pesetsky's house.

She flung the door open clad in a crème-colored silk bathrobe and monogrammed slippers.

Spittle formed at the edges of her mouth as she swore at us when we presented our search warrant. "You'll pay for this. I'm calling my attorney right now."

"Good idea," I said.

She stormed down the hallway and slammed the door to what I assumed was her bedroom.

Stan and I gloved up and started in the kitchen. We were working our way through her collection of cookware when she emerged in full makeup, dressed in a jet-black pant-suit and heels, every frosted hair in place. "I'm off to see Mark Goldman, my attorney. You'll be hearing from him. Count on it."

I nodded and she stalked off, her heels clicking on the parquet floor of her entryway.

When she slammed the door closed, Stan turned to me. "Goldman's one slick lawyer. Should we be worried?"

I pushed aside her Cuisinart and pulled out the small

gadget behind it and held it up for Stan to see. "She's the one who should be worried. Let's bag this sucker. Maybe we'll finally get lucky."

We continued searching her condo for the next several hours. No gun, but at least we'd found her pill grinder. We dropped it off with Tony at the lab and begged him to do a rush job. He promised he'd get right on it.

By this time, it was mid-afternoon. Stan and I were starving and headed for Wendy's. I checked my messages and saw three from Dr. Stein.

"Shit. I completely blanked my therapy appointment. I'm mortified."

"Well, this case has been a little distracting," Stan said.

"Still, I feel terrible." I punched in Dr. Stein's number and got her answering machine. She must be with another client. I apologized profusely and promised to reschedule and pay for the missed appointment.

As Stan and I munched on our sandwiches and fries, he said, "I've got a good feeling about this."

"You do?"

"Yeah. We've gone through so much crap on this case we're due for something breaking our way."

"God, I hope you're right, Stan. I am so ready for some good news."

———

That night, Hank called. "Having a great week with Jack, but I miss you."

"I miss you, too," I said, and realized it was true.

We chatted for a few minutes and made plans for another Sunday night dinner date. "You pick the place this time," Hank said.

"How about you come to dinner here? I make a pretty good lasagna—my grandmother's recipe."

"You're on. Seven good?"

It suddenly occurred to me that Hank might think this was an invitation to more than dinner. I wasn't ready for a sleepover. "Uh, yeah. Actually, could we do six? I'll have to kick you out by eight. Stan and I have early stuff to do Monday morning."

"I can do that," he said, sounding uncertain.

What was I doing? I needed to be straight with this guy. I hesitated, then said, "Truthfully, all I'm ready for right now is dinner. I think I'm still recovering from my last…entanglement."

"Hey, just dinner with you sounds great. Taking things slow works for me. And I don't want you to worry. I'm not going to try to jump your bones."

I laughed. "Jump my bones? What are we—in high school?"

"When I'm with you, I feel like I'm back there, falling for the statuesque girl my eyes want to follow everywhere she goes."

"Statuesque, huh? Sounds a lot better than tall and gangly."

"We're going to have to work on your self-esteem, Caitlin O'Connor. Your self-image is seriously out of whack."

"You think so?"

"Oh yeah."

———

The call from Tony came the next afternoon. "I think I may have found what you're looking for. The pill grinder has traces of nitroglycerin on it."

"You're kidding," I said. "Thank you, thank you! We owe you a pizza."

"With the works?"

"Definitely."

I turned to Stan and gave him the good news.

"You think it's enough?"

"Let's hope so. Come on. I think we should talk to the captain."

We rushed down the hall and knocked on Captain Singleton's door.

When he looked up and peered at us through the glass partition, he waved us in with a frown. "What now, you two?"

"The lab results just came back, Captain. Traces of nitroglycerin were on the pill grinder in Sarah Pesetsky's kitchen. We wanted to check with you. Do you think we have enough for an arrest? She insists she can explain the phone calls from Gus and the money she withdrew. Claims she was loaning money to Gus for his wife's treatment and has no idea why he wanted it in cash. But Gus's wife doesn't think he ever would have asked her for a loan. I think she'd be willing to testify."

He leaned his elbows on his desk and his chin in his hands and stared at me, then Stan, a bleak look on his face. "Let me talk to the DA, see what he thinks. If we do this, we need to drop all the charges against Victor Pesetsky. The press will have a field day. I can see the headlines now: 'Bumbling police falsely accuse celebrated ballet director of lurid murder of his ballerina wife.' Civil suit, here we come."

"I really am so sorry, sir, but we have a chance here to close two murder cases, Gus's and Lydia Miseau's."

He twisted his lips and looked up to the ceiling. "Well, there is that. Let me get back to you two, okay?"

# FORTY-ONE

Sarah Pesetsky pressed her fingers against her forehead. Her head throbbed, which she was determined to ignore. She booted up her computer and looked up an address. As she scribbled it down, Jackie called her name. She jumped.

"Didn't mean to startle you," she said. "I was just wondering whether you wanted me to load these boxes in your car to take to Goodwill."

"No, not right now. I... I have something I need to do. Maybe later, Jackie." Sarah jumped up, grabbed her purse and coat, and hurried out the door. She'd stop at her bank first and visit her safe deposit box. Just in case.

Half an hour later, Sarah left the bank and realized she'd forgotten to bring the address she'd looked up. She called Jackie and explained she'd left the slip of paper by her computer with her friend's address on it.

"Found it." Jackie recited the address to her.

Sarah repeated it back and hurriedly hung up.

# FORTY-TWO

I was surprised when I got a call within the hour, not from Captain Singleton, but from the DA himself. In his usual booming voice, Barclay bellowed, "O'Connor, I can't say I'm thrilled that you apparently arrested the wrong guy for Miseau's murder. He's a major player in the arts community, you know. But I think we can spin this that your investigation into the Mikowski shooting led you to new evidence, and you and Bisso, dedicated public servants, were determined to get to the truth."

Actually, that didn't sound like spin to me so much as what had actually happened. But I wasn't about to say that to Barclay. The guy was like a miniature pit bull who didn't like to be challenged.

"That sounds good. So, it's a go to arrest her?"

"Faxing the warrant over. Once we get her into custody, I'll put the order in to drop the charges against Victor Pesetsky. I figure once he collects on Lydia's insurance, he'll be more forgiving."

"Let's hope so, sir."

When we got to Sarah Pesetsky's condo, Jackie answered the door. "Oh, you two again. I'm sorry. Ms. Pesetsky went out."

"Do you have any idea where?"

"She said she had something she needed to do. Left in an awful hurry. But she called me to read her this address she forgot to take." Jackie went over to the computer and picked up a slip of paper and handed it to me.

My stomach dropped when I recognized Mary Mikowski's address. "Stan, we need to go. Now."

Stan took one look at my face and joined me as we raced out of the house and into our car.

"You drive," I said and gave him the address. "She's gone to see Mary Mikowski. I can't imagine she'd be crazy enough to hurt her, but if she thinks Mary knows anything, who knows what she'll do?"

I pulled out my phone and searched for Mary's number, and then punched it in.

There was no answer.

# FORTY-THREE

We'd called for backup, but none had arrived by the time we pulled up in front of Mary's flat. Stan double-parked and put his flashers on, as I raced up the porch steps and banged on the door. No answer.

I pounded on the door. Hard. "Mary, I know you're in there. Let me in."

Finally, the door opened a crack.

Half of Mary's pinched face peered out at me. "This isn't a good time, Lieutenant. I'm sorry." Her voice sounded unnaturally high. She moved to close the door and I wedged my foot in to stop her.

Stan had joined me and stood by the side of the door, out of sight with his gun drawn. I gestured for him to wait there. No sense in escalating the situation if we didn't have to.

"I'm coming in, Mary. I just want to make sure you're okay."

"No, don't," she cried.

I pushed my way through the door and came face to face with Mary who stood shaking, breathing hard. Sarah Pesetsky had one hand clamped around her neck, while the other held a gun jammed against her head.

"Sarah, I need you to let Mary go and put the gun down," I said, trying to keep my voice calm.

"Oh, I don't think so, Lieutenant. Mary didn't seem to believe I'd loaned Gus money. And to think it was all to help her. Isn't that a shame?"

"I don't know what she's talking about," Mary cried. "I tried to tell her I don't know anything."

"It's okay, Mary." My gaze fastened on Sarah. "Don't make things worse for yourself. Put the gun down now." I took a step forward.

"Come any closer, and I'll be forced to shoot the little widow here."

"You don't need to do this. Mary doesn't know anything. She can't hurt you."

"But you can." She pushed Mary away and pointed her gun directly at me.

The last thing I heard before she pulled the trigger was the sound of Stan moving behind me, screaming, "No!"

# FORTY-FOUR

Getting shot pretty much sucked. I knew I shouldn't complain because Stan rushing in and screaming had apparently distracted Sarah enough to throw off her aim. She got my shoulder instead of my heart. Of course, now I was spending more time rehabbing it with my physical therapist than I was at my desk at work.

And working a desk job was where I was stuck until I was cleared to return to active duty.

Sarah Pesetsky wasn't so lucky. Stan's aim was a lot better than hers, and he took her out as she was about to turn her gun on Mary. Thanks to Mary's testimony, the shooting was ruled justified, but not before, as Stan later told me, he went through hours of interrogation and required meetings with the shrink the department brought in.

"If anything happened to you, Cait, that would have been it. I would have lost it. Started drinking again." We were sitting in my living room with huge mugs of coffee my first day out of the hospital.

I pointed at my sling. "Something did happen to me, and you didn't drink. And you probably saved my life roaring in there, not to mention Mary's."

"Why the hell did you want me to wait and not come in with you?" he asked.

"I thought I could handle it, talk her down. But she'd gone way over the edge. Bad call on my part."

"No kidding."

"Hey, no picking on the wounded here."

"Okay, okay." He glanced around my living room. "You think you've got enough flowers in here? Your place looks like a funeral parlor."

I grinned. "Melissa, my mom, and Hank went a little crazy. They're beautiful, don't you think?"

"Whoa, whoa, whoa. Who the hell is Hank?"

"I've told you about him, haven't I?"

"I don't think so."

"No? Well, he's this really nice guy who teaches middle school. I met him through Melissa. We've gone out a few times."

"He's not married, is he?'

I picked up a throw pillow with my good hand and threw it at him. "No! I'm in recovery. Remember?"

"How could I forget? Partners fighting crime and our addictions. We're quite a pair. So, when do I get to meet this paragon?"

"Soon."

———

Something had shifted between Hank and me ever since the shooting. Maybe it reminded both of us that life was fragile, and there were no guarantees. But now all that discussion of taking things really slowly... well, it seemed a bit beside the point.

When he came to see me at the hospital, bearing an enormous bouquet of spring flowers, he couldn't resist teasing me. "Geez, Cait, I knew you were worried about having me over to dinner, but you didn't have to go this far to get out of it."

It was the first time I'd really smiled since everything had gone down at Mary's flat. "I promise to make you lasagna, but you'll have to take me out for a while. It's hard to cook with a bum shoulder."

"Or you could come over to my place for dinner. I make a mean chicken marsala."

"Really?"

"Well, no, actually, my mom makes a mean chicken marsala. But I can read and follow her directions."

"You can think of it as a science experiment, and I know you're good at those."

He took my good hand and kissed my fingers. Then he lifted his head, and his gaze held mine. "I am," he said.

After that, he called or came by every day, and without even discussing it, we seemed to drift into a lovely "He's with me, and I'm with her" stage in our relationship. On the weeks he didn't have Jack, either he came over to my house, or I came over to his after work.

One night, we were snuggling on my living room couch listening to Ella Fitzgerald sing "Nice Work If You Can Get It" when Hank nuzzled my neck and said, "I have something to tell you. You know how I said I was always reluctant to have Jack meet anybody I went out with?"

"I'm aware," I said, carefully.

"Well, I told him all about you. He wants to meet you."

My heart thumped wildly in my chest. "Really?"

"Really."

"I'm like… so happy. But scared, too. What if he doesn't like me?"

He rolled his eyes. "I've heard about how you are with Melissa's kids. She says you're a natural kid magnet. I'm not worried."

"That makes one of us. But I still can't wait to meet him."

Meantime, Stan and I had apparently wormed our way back into Captain's good graces, probably because both he and the DA were reveling in all the publicity about how these "courageous detectives" had managed to foil this mad woman who apparently had killed her ex-husband's wife, her blackmailer, and had been on the verge of killing the blackmailer's innocent widow. Gerald Gladstone's death never came up, but I still suspected Sarah had a hand in her father's death as well.

Requests for interviews poured in, but Stan and I refused all of them. He didn't want to talk about the shooting, and I didn't want to go there either. I think we both just wanted to get back to some semblance of normalcy.

Dr. Stein had been helping me cope with my flashbacks, and Stan was still seeing the shrink who'd interviewed him after the shooting—only not professionally. She turned out to be a very attractive divorcée a few years older than Stan, with two kids. It was obvious he was totally smitten. And vice versa.

What a hell of a year it had been for both Stan and me. And yet, we'd survived, and things were getting better.

Even Mary Mikowski was hanging in there, although when I visited her, she confided her dismay about learning that Gus had resorted to blackmail to pay for her treatments. "I just can't get over it," she told me, as we sat drinking tea in her duplex. "He was such a good man. Why would he have done something like that? He never had so much as a parking ticket."

"I think he felt desperate. He didn't want to lose you, and he lost perspective."

She shook her head. "If only he'd talked to me. I never would have let him do something crazy like this."

I put my hand over her frail one. "I hope you can focus on how much he loved you and all your good memories of your lives together."

"I'm trying."

"You do look better, Mary." She had more color in her cheeks.

She brightened. "You know, I think these treatments are helping."

"Gus would be so glad you went ahead with them."

"I know. I miss him so much, and I'm so mad at him for throwing his life away like he did—throwing our lives away."

"Sometimes the people we care about do crazy things in the name of love."

"Well, let me tell you, if I get to see Gus again in the after-life, he's going to hear one earful from me."

"I don't doubt it," I said.

# FORTY-FIVE

Three weeks later, I drove to Ballet Études. Amazingly, Dora, the receptionist, was still there, wearing a tie-dyed orange and purple granny dress and combat boots, with her hair dyed back to matching amber and violet streaks. Talk about being color coordinated.

"You're still here," I said. "Last time I saw you, you were looking for another job."

She grinned. "Things are much better, now that Victor's been cleared." She lowered her voice. "I think the company must have gotten a windfall or something. No layoffs, and Victor even gave me a raise."

Apparently, the insurance company had finally paid up. "Is Victor in?" I asked.

"Yeah, I think he's in his office."

"Thanks." I headed downstairs and down the hall, not at all sure he wouldn't throw me out the moment he saw me.

When I tentatively knocked on his door, he looked up and his eyes widened, as he gestured for me to come in. "Lieutenant O'Connor, I didn't expect to see you again. What brings you here?" His face looked more deeply lined than I remembered. I supposed losing your wife and getting falsely accused of murder can leave its mark.

I took a seat and licked my lips. "I came to apologize. I shouldn't have jumped the gun and arrested you for something you didn't do. I'm sorry."

He gave me a long look. Finally, he said, "You were just doing your job, Lieutenant. In your shoes, I would have thought I was the likeliest suspect as well."

I leaned forward. "Did you have any idea that your ex-wife could have done something like this?"

He shook his head. "I knew she was bitter about the divorce even after all these years. But I never imagined she would take it out on Lydia and try to destroy me as well. Frederick says he thinks she went off the deep end when she was doing the photography project, saw how everyone worshipped Lydia. Raked it all back up for her."

I was shocked to see his eyes redden. I wanted to comfort him. "At least everyone knows now that you're innocent. That must be a relief to you."

He took his glasses off and rubbed his eyes. "I'm not really innocent, you know. I hurt Sarah terribly. I neglected my own children, and I wasn't a very good husband to Lydia either. All these years, the company, my work, was all I really cared about. Now I must live with the consequences of my own single-mindedness."

"I really am sorry. For everything."

"Ah, we both have regrets, you and I. But perhaps, we can do better."

I thought about all I regretted—falsely accusing Victor, my obsession with my reputation as a crack detective, not to mention my ill-fated relationship with a married man. "I certainly want to do that."

He stood up and held his hand out to shake mine. "I hope you won't be too offended if I tell you that I sincerely wish I won't see you ever again."

"Well, I do have a subscription for your next season."

———

It was another six months before Hank and I paid a return visit to the aquarium. We were sitting on the side wall of the Touch Habitat discussing what to make for dinner when Jack raced over and grabbed my hand with his wet one. "Caitlin, come on! Come pet this baby shark with me. I'm making friends with him."

Hank groused, "What about me?"

"You can come too, Dad."

Hank grinned at me, and we walked over to the sharks, arm in arm.

I gamely stuck my hand in the icy water and tried not to make a face as I petted the baby shark.

"Isn't this cool?" Jack said. The shark swam away.

I gazed at him, then at Hank, not believing my good fortune in having these two amazing guys in my life.

"Very cool," I said. "Let's pet him again when he comes back around."

THE END

———

**Don't miss out on your next favorite book!**
**Join the Melange Books mailing list at**
www.melange-books.com / mail.html

# ACKNOWLEDGMENTS

What a pleasure to once again have the opportunity to work with Nancy Schumacher and Caroline Andrus at Melange Books, as well as my editor Sybelle Maloney, who made this a much better book. The multi-gifted Caroline Andrus once again designed the cover. I am one lucky writer.

I'm also so grateful to the folks who offered both encouragement and constructive feedback, most especially Ellen Birkett Morris, Mary Popham, and Whitney Vale of North End Writers, as well as Virginia Van Pelt, Connie Bergstein Dow, and Elaine Munsch who read early versions of *Missed Cue* and offered valuable suggestions.

*Missed Cue* grew out of a short story I contributed to Malice Domestic's *Murder Most Theatrical.* A shoutout to friend and fellow writer Beth Schmelzer who challenged me to write a story for the anthology. Special thanks as well to Luci Hansson Zahray, aka "the Poison Lady," for her expert advice.

I'm also so grateful to Simone Jung at Books Forward for helping me get the word out about MISSED CUE.

Finally, I'm thankful for my amazing husband Alan, always my first reader and encourager-in-chief.

## THANK YOU FOR READING

Did you enjoy this book?

We invite you to leave a review at the website of your choice, such as Goodreads, Amazon, Barnes & Noble, etc.

### DID YOU KNOW THAT LEAVING A REVIEW...

- Helps other readers find books they may enjoy.
- Gives you a chance to let your voice be heard.
- Gives authors recognition for their hard work.
- Doesn't have to be long. A sentence or two about why you liked the book will do.

# ABOUT THE AUTHOR

**Lynn Slaughter** is addicted to chocolate, the arts, and her husband's cooking. After a long career as a professional dancer and dance educator, she earned her MFA in Writing Popular Fiction from Seton Hill University.

Her previous award-winning novels include *Deadly Setup* and *Leisha's Song*, both published by Fire and Ice/Melange Books. She is also the author of *It Should Have Been You*, a Silver Falchion finalist, and *While I Danced*, an EPIC finalist.

The ridiculously proud mother of two sons and grandmother of five, she lives in Louisville, Kentucky where she is at work on her next novel and is an active member and former president of Derby Rotten Scoundrels, her local Sisters in Crime chapter. She loves hearing from readers and hopes you'll visit her website, www.lynnslaughter.com.

lynnslaughter.com/blog

 twitter.com/lslaughter2

# ALSO BY LYNN SLAUGHTER